THIS BOOK'S JACKET, and twelve full-color illustrations, are enhanced with interactive augmented reality that you can experience by downloading a free app to your phone or tablet.

Download the free app at betweenworldsapp.com, point your device at the art, then take this story to the next level—with 3-D characters that can teach you magic . . . or battle techniques.

Available for iOS and Android

SKIP BRITTENHAM

BETWEEN WORLDS

with art by
JAY ANACLETO
BRIAN HABERLIN
DOUG SIROIS

G. P. Putnam's Sons

G. P. PUTNAM'S SONS
an imprint of Penguin Random House LLC
375 Hudson Street, New York, NY 10014

Library of Congress Cataloging-in-Publication Data is available upon request.

Printed in the United States of America.
ISBN 978-0-399-17689-0
1 3 5 7 9 10 8 6 4 2

Design by Ryan Thomann. Text set in Fiesole.

For the love of my life, Heather,
who inspired me to write;

my fabulous daughters, Kristina, Shauna, and India,
who encouraged me to keep going;

and my buddy Tom,
who never lets me forget how important it is to have fun.

PROLOGUE

AFTER THE LITTLE GIRL'S FUNERAL, the mourners crowded together in her parents' living room. A cloud of regret hung in the air like an impending storm, masking the fragrance of the traditional white lilies that filled the room. Dozens of tribute posters handcrafted by Laura's classmates hung in neat rows above the mantelpiece.

But neither art nor words of sympathy could diminish the pain of Laura's heartbroken parents. Their other child, a twelve-year-old boy named Aaron, huddled on a chair in the corner of the living room, his red hair standing out like a flag against his ashen skin.

A few days ago, he'd started a snowball fight with his little sister Laura at a local park. To escape the rain of snowballs Aaron was hurling, Laura had bolted out onto the snow-covered ice on the surface of the park's pond—she couldn't tell that there was water beneath her feet because the heavy snow had erased any definable shore.

The ice cracked and Laura fell through. Aaron yelled for help, but no one was nearby. He quickly slid on his belly out onto the frozen pond, until he was right in front of the open hole. Aaron couldn't make out Laura's bright purple jacket under the jagged pieces of ice, but he plunged his arms deep into the frigid water and felt desperately for her, screaming her name. His hands couldn't find any part of her. He continued to scream and splash long after he knew it was too late.

Now a steady stream of family friends and classmates shuffled toward his corner, trying to comfort him, all making a point of emphasizing that it wasn't his fault. But their words only tormented him: they knew and he knew that it could only be his fault. He should have been protecting her, not hitting her with snowballs.

Mary, a friend of Aaron's mom, walked over and put a hand on his shoulder, then crouched so she was at his eye level. "You did your best," she said, wiping away the tears and mascara that trailed down her face. "It was just . . . her time."

But it *shouldn't* have been her time. Aaron vaulted to his feet, swept past Mary's legs, then pushed clumsily through the cluster of mourners. He plucked his black winter parka from a wooden peg near the front door and hastily put it on, then opened the door to an arctic blast and a cold, bleak landscape.

Aaron's mother had been sitting on a couch with her head in her hands, weeping, but she looked up when she felt the cold air rushing in. "Where are you going, Aaron?" she called out feebly. It was all well and good for her to wonder what he was doing *now*, but she and his father had been holed up in their bedroom for days, ignoring him and crying together. He knew they didn't want him anymore—not after what he'd done to Laura.

Without replying, Aaron walked out into the bitter Minnesota midwinter cold and closed the door behind him. He grabbed the handlebars of his blue Electra cruiser, which was leaning against the deck, and used the pair of fur-lined leather gloves he pulled from his pockets to slap the snow off the seat.

The curtains were pulled open by a handful of wide-eyed adults, who stared out at him. Aaron flipped up the hood of his parka, mounted the bike, and pedaled around the parked cars and down the snow-covered driveway, then turned onto the slushy country road.

Powdery white snowflakes were falling, but the ominous gray sky boiling above him foreshadowed more severe weather on the way. His teary eyes made the pine trees blur into vague masses of green and brown that streamed past him as he raced down the road. Aaron didn't have any particular destination in mind; he just needed to find a way to stop thinking about how guilty he felt—at least for a while.

A half hour later, the wheels of his bike skittered into a gravel parking lot pockmarked with lumps of ice and snow. The fast-paced ride had made him sweaty, and the white dress shirt he'd worn to the funeral was sticking to his skin. As he stepped off the bike, a gust of wind enveloped him, sending a chill down his spine. He reached down and zipped the parka to his chin.

A battered gray split-rail fence with two yellow NO TRES-PASSING signs lined the edge of a large open meadow carpeted with patches of snow. Next to the fence, a log pole bore a cracked wooden sign, which read MYSTERY FOREST VIEWING AREA. Underneath it was a MYSTERY FOREST LEGENDS sign.

A shabby rangers' log cabin sat at the west end of the "viewing area," but the windows were dark, and it appeared to be as unoccupied as the parking lot.

Aaron wiped his nose with the back of his hand and looked around. He had no idea what had drawn him there. The town council had attached the word *Mystery* to the aspen grove over a decade ago, in a lame attempt to create a tourist attraction. There was nothing mysterious about the Mystery Forest, though—it was just a big aspen grove that butted against an old-growth pine forest.

The council encouraged the townspeople to create and circulate rumors about the grove, anyway, and the town and local paper had adopted the task with enthusiasm. Of the tales that had emerged—the dumbest and most improbable one—was that a Wishing Tree lived at the grove's center. If it was in the right mood, the Tree would grant a wish to whoever touched it. As far as Aaron knew, no one had ever found the Tree, much less had a wish granted . . . probably because it didn't *exist*. After numerous hikers trying to find the Tree or unearth the "mystery" had become lost or required rescue, Forest Service officials severely reduced access by requiring hikers to apply for special entry permits, which were rarely granted.

Eventually, the myth of the Tree died, along with the town's other fanciful forest stories. The smattering of people who still came here did so to photograph the herds of pewter-colored mule deer that the rangers lured into the meadow with grain and fresh hay.

The Tree might not be real, but Aaron desperately wanted to believe that *something* could alter his sister's fate—and his. Ignoring the NO TRESPASSING signs, he climbed over the sagging fence and tramped toward the pine forest at the meadow's end. After crossing the rickety covered bridge that spanned the slowly meandering river, he finally reached the tree line. His heart began to pound, and his mouth went dry. Aaron clenched his fists into tight balls and took a step into the forest. No matter how improbable his quest for the Tree was, he felt compelled to trespass into the forbidden forest to continue it.

The snow danced wildly in the wind and began to fall harder, quickly covering the trails like lacy white curtains. Not knowing which way to go, Aaron dashed into the largest open space between the trees and began to march through the woods. Soon, heavy clumps of slush caked his boots, making every step harder, but he couldn't stop, and he definitely couldn't go home.

Before long, the huge stands of green pine, fir, and spruce disappeared. Only a wall of aspen trees remained: tall and regal, with bright white trunks streaked with black. They crowded close together, like the Red Queen's soldiers standing at attention. *Good*, Aaron thought, his spirits lifting. He was actually in the Mystery Forest where he needed to be, and maybe something . . . better . . . would happen. Whether he found the Tree or not, the walk would distract him. Either way, it was better than being at the wake.

A half hour later, as dusk neared, a searing blast of wind slapped his face, burnishing the raw pink marks on his cheeks. He was weary and disoriented, and his pace had slowed to a depressing trudge. The temperature was continuing to dip, and he felt his first real pulse of fear. He *was* lost, like all those other hikers.

In this section of the grove, the aspens grew closer together, making his passage even more difficult. Their skeletal branches swayed in the dim light, vaguely menacing, as though warning him to turn back. Nevertheless, he kept forcing choppy, determined steps out of his weary legs.

After several more minutes of plodding, he noticed that the snow had stopped falling. Then he realized that the slush he'd been walking through was thinning. Aaron continued to weave between the aspens, drawn ever onward by an inner strength he hadn't known he possessed. A mild breeze stroked his sore cheeks, like a warm current in the ocean. He turned his head around, and it was cold again, then moved his face back toward the warmth and followed his feet in that direction.

He'd been picking his way through the trees for so long, it

took him a moment to realize that he'd finally come to a clearing. In its center stood a solitary aspen, its bright white bark glistening in the twilight. The circumference of its trunk was huge: it was as if dozens of aspens had been fused together to create a Goliath. The tree was so tall and so wide, with such a multitude of branches, that Aaron couldn't see its top, even with his head tilted all the way back. This was absolutely the biggest tree he'd ever seen.

If there *was* a Wishing Tree, this had to be it. At this point, he had nothing to lose by trying. Aaron pulled off his soggy gloves and stroked the trunk, which was surprisingly warm. The wood seemed to pulse, as though it had a heartbeat of its own.

Maybe the Tree *could* do magic. Tears rushed to Aaron's eyes as he thought about how much he missed Laura. He would never forget the last time he saw her, laughing as she ran out onto the ice. He leaned against the tree and slid his hands along the trunk until he was sitting. Aaron was bone-weary, and his eyelids were growing heavy. He yawned—then yawned again. Feeling like he needed to close his eyes, just for a minute, he scooped out a hollow in the leaves so he could lie down with his head next to the Tree.

None of the stories he'd heard revealed how to make a particular wish come true. Maybe just really *wanting* it to come true was enough. He stretched his palms over his head so he could touch the warm bark, and wished for the Tree to bring his sister back to life.

Then, right before his consciousness slipped away, he added a postscript: "If you can't bring her back, please take me *far away*, to a place where no one will know me and I can do something to make up for my mistake."

As Aaron drifted off, golden leaves from the giant aspen—which *should* have been bare like all the other trees—fell from the branches, then swirled around him on a warm wind before rising back into the air.

Aaron's eyelids fluttered. Once. Then again. The first thing he remembered was that Laura was dead. Then he remembered it was his fault. He leaped to his feet as he recalled the hike through the forest and falling asleep next to the gigantic tree.

He looked up through the thick branches of the Wishing Tree, shading his eyes from the bright sunlight that filtered through. Surely only a few hours had passed, but there was no trace of winter, and the ground was bone-dry. The air had gone from frigid to warm to humid—hot, even. It had to be hot, he thought, to have melted the snow so fast—but he couldn't have slept *that* long. He stripped off his heavy parka and tied its arms snugly around his waist. His sleep-addled brain jerked awkwardly back to life as his senses confirmed that it wasn't winter anymore. The giant tree—and the other aspens—were adorned with the full green leaves of summer. He smelled fresh grass and heard the hum of insects.

"Laura," he cried.

Leaves rustled, but no one replied.

He yelled again, louder, "Laura!"

The pocket of solace he had enjoyed while sleeping under the Tree evaporated. *Something* had happened, but certainly the most important part of his wish hadn't been granted, because there was no sign of his sister.

He plunged into the aspen forest as quickly as his unsteady legs allowed, tacking away from the Wishing Tree and through the tightly packed aspens. About ten minutes later, he broke from the cover of the grove and entered a lush meadow without ever having passed through the pine forest, which made no sense at all. A few feet into the meadow, he stopped and gaped. Acres and acres of land were blanketed with thick, green, shoulder-high grass.

Thunderstruck, Aaron stared at the meadow, not sure if he was dreaming or hallucinating. A clump of grass near his right boot stirred, and a mound of moist earth began to rise. A green and white head with too many eyes poked out of the dirt. At first glance, it appeared to be a large salamander, but then it used long claws at the ends of three sets of front legs to dig out its hindquarters, which revealed six additional sets of legs. Its eyes slid over Aaron as it paddled out of the hole, slithered over his boot like a centipede, then rapidly dug and vanished into a hole on the boot's other side.

A loud whomping sound distracted Aaron from what had just happened at his feet. A large shadow swept over his head, and the air was pierced by a high-pitched shriek. Then a huge, fiery red *something* was swooping down with leathery wings pulled in tight, hugging its belly. The wings extended with a loud *whap*, slowing the creature's dive as it stretched razor-sharp yellow talons toward him. Aaron dove into the grass just as a talon ripped through his shirt, raking out a line of flesh. The rest of the creature's talons closed on empty air.

As adrenaline spiked his brain, he rolled onto his feet and sprinted back to the safety of the aspens. The canopy protected him from further assault, but he still heard the creature's wings thundering in the distance.

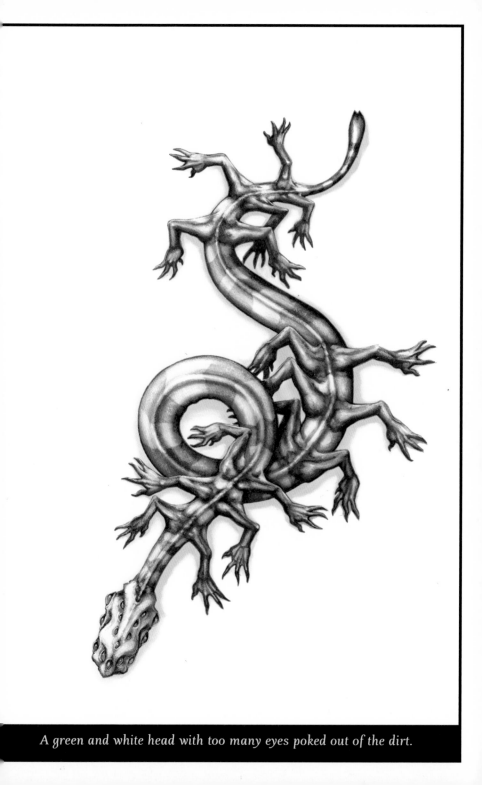

A green and white head with too many eyes poked out of the dirt.

CHAPTER 1

MAYBERRY SLOUCHED in one of Eden Grove High's straight-backed wooden auditorium seats, so bored she was almost ready for an electrolyte IV and an oxygen mask to revive her fading mind.

She wore a baggy gray Southern Death Cult tee, paired with black cargo pants embellished with metallic zippers, clips, and buckles—an outfit that deliberately revealed nothing about her figure. Her glossy black hair was cut into an angular bob, with bright purple streaks. Below her right eye she sported a black-lined curlicue temporary tattoo of her own creation, and her maroon lipstick went nicely with her jet-black fingernails and precisely drawn eyebrows. She was totally out of place in Eden Grove, Minnesota, where the girls went for a look that was more Kardashian than Blondie.

Any sensible teenager who'd just moved to a new town

would have edited her style to match the local dress code, but Mayberry was stubborn and sometimes more impulsive than sensible. She hated the idea that she had to conform in order to make friends, and her mom's frequent urging to do so didn't make the idea any more palatable. She rolled her head back and stared dully at the auditorium's ceiling.

After Mayberry was born, her mother had taken a hiatus from Columbia University's doctoral program so she could be a full-time parent. Now that Mayberry was fifteen—too old to want or need full-time supervision—the family had moved from New York City to rural Minnesota so her mom could finally finish her thesis. The subject of her doctorate was the pathology of northern aspens, and the forests she'd chosen to study were all within a day's drive of Eden Grove. Her dad hadn't minded the move, since he owned a small software service company and could work from anywhere. Mayberry questioned her mom's timing—why couldn't she just wait until Mayberry was out of the house and in college?

Mayberry might have been . . . quirky . . . but in Manhattan, friends had surrounded her. She'd been going to school with the same group since first grade, and made new friends at local shows and theater performances. There were plenty of like-minded free spirits in Manhattan, and being born there had only helped Mayberry's prospects. She might not have known much about the natural world or outdoor life, but she was a walking subway map.

She'd gradually shied away from her usual social scene,

though, after her parents told her about the impending move. Leaving the only home she had ever known loomed over her like a guillotine's blade. Her best friend, Emily, had stuck around, but her sort-of boyfriend, Peter, had gradually distanced himself. Even though she'd known that they'd never manage a long-distance relationship, she'd never been more heartbroken than when she learned that he and Emily had hooked up. There were angry texts and tearful phone calls between the girls, and for now, they weren't talking. Even more disturbing was the fact that none of her other friends had chosen to jump in and defend her or pop their quills out to skewer Peter and Emily for their betrayal. They had all taken Emily's side, as if Mayberry didn't count anymore, and started keeping their distance, too.

Mayberry's spirit needed a boost, but if there was a more mind-numbing, backward place to get it than Eden Grove, she couldn't imagine where. Nevertheless, here she sat, patiently waiting for a chance to carve a fit-in-with-the-locals niche by auditioning for a small part in the school's upcoming Autumn Chorale production. She was a pretty good singer and had performed in her school's plays for as long as she could remember. Theater geeks were usually a good starting place when it came to finding friends.

Except for Kylie Murphy. Mayberry couldn't categorize *her* as a theater geek. She was more of an archetypal mean girl. Kylie was currently standing in the middle of the auditorium's stage, her arms flung up and out, warbling Céline

Dion's "Taking Chances." She belted it out like a beauty-contest contestant showing off her new "talent," trying to squeeze an entire song's worth of emotion into every line.

Mayberry grimaced at Kylie's pitch—the girl sounded like a parrot getting crushed in a wood chipper. To keep her mind off the unholy sounds coming from the stage, Mayberry doodled a caricature of Kylie on her sketch pad. She smiled as she drew a giraffe's neck, chunky hippo body, twisted mouth, and bugged-out saucer eyes. Mayberry had always liked creating fantastical animals, and seeing another side of Kylie on the page was particularly satisfying.

CHAPTER 2

MAYBERRY TUGGED her vibrating cell phone from the front pocket of her cargos. Her friend Marshall— so far, her *only* real friend in Minnesota—had texted. He'd been one of the first people to talk to her, and seemed to appreciate all the things about her that made others think she was weird—her geeking out on science, love of punk music, odd choice of clothes, and sometimes snarky attitude.

She glanced over her shoulder and spotted him in the auditorium's last row, his worn red Converse propped on the empty seat in front of him. A gray T-shirt and scruffy plaid pullover hung loosely from his six-foot frame, making it look like he'd plucked them at random from a donation box on the curb outside a thrift store. *Bad fashion call*, she thought. Marshall was almost cute, with brown eyes, a strong jawline, and choppy blond hair, but his cowlicks made him look like he'd just rolled out of a pile of hay. Oversized brown glasses completed the nondescript look, making him the perfect contestant for a makeover show.

His text was made up of the shorthand they'd developed: **SSS**. *She so sucks.*

UGTR, she texted back. *You got that right.*

Kylie finished demolishing the song, then dipped her knees and raised an arm in an awkward curtsy. Her best friend, Penny Singleton, began applauding and hooting loudly, then the rest of their clique joined in, feigning the kind of excitement that would come over a crowd if Beyoncé had just performed an original ballad. Penny finally lowered her hands to smooth her hair, then absentmindedly plucked balls of fluff from her tight pink sweater, which flowed smoothly into a form-fitting gray miniskirt. She wouldn't need to change even one piece of her outfit if she were called upon to play a Pink Lady in *Grease.*

Penny and Mayberry hadn't started out on the right foot, to say the least. Trouble had the bad habit of plucking Mayberry from a crowd. Although, to be totally fair to Trouble, she sometimes seemed to seek him out. Case in point: When Mayberry passed Penny and her friends in the hallway during her first week of school, Penny sneered at her, then turned away and whispered to her friends, who giggled while staring daggers at the new girl. Mayberry knew Penny's type. If she didn't stand up for herself right away, she'd be doing the girl's homework before the year was out. Without missing a beat, she stepped over and put her face so close to Penny's that she could see the flakes of mascara on her lashes.

"Do we have a problem?" Mayberry whispered, as if she were telling her a secret.

"What?" Penny said, aghast, shuffling back a step. "No . . . I don't . . . I mean, why would we?"

"Good. Have a nice day," Mayberry chirped, narrowing her eyes into threatening slits before spinning around and walking away. From that moment on, the two of them were in a cold war that sometimes seemed on the verge of turning hot. Either way, after the confrontation, Mayberry didn't talk to Penny or her friends or they to her. Mayberry realized that she might have gone too far, but it was too late to backpedal.

She'd managed to befriend a few of the girls who weren't fans of Penny or her minions, but she only really *liked* hanging out with Marshall. He would have been cuter if he wasn't such a dork, but either way, he was definitely not her type, mostly because he was so timid. If he was bullied, which he often was, Marshall ignored it instead of standing up for himself.

"Mayberry Hansen," screeched the music teacher, Miss Speca. Her voice had a disconcerting edge to it, like the point of a nail being dragged across sheet metal. That unsettling sound was still reverberating in Mayberry's mind as she rose and forced a smile. She strode up the aisle toward the stage, pointedly ignoring Penny and her friends.

"What is that freak grinning at?" Penny whispered, just loud enough for Mayberry to hear. "There aren't any mirrors in the auditorium, so she can't see how ridiculous her clothes look."

Mayberry raised an eyebrow and turned to Penny. "Actually, I'm thinking about how ridiculous *you* look," she said, waving an arm at Penny's tiny miniskirt and platform heels.

Mayberry skipped up the steps to the stage as Penny's lips twisted into a sulky frown.

"Let's sing, shall we?" Miss Speca said from her seat at the piano bench.

"I'm ready when you are, Miss Speca," Mayberry trilled. "You should have the music already."

Miss Speca's bony fingers thumped out the opening chords of the David Gray song "Sail Away" while Mayberry focused on remembering the words. The first notes of the song came out fresh and pure. Although Mayberry could still hear Penny tittering, she tried to stay calm by imagining herself in an old-fashioned nightclub, performing for an audience of red-lipsticked ladies and their dapper escorts.

Then there was a loud snort and she heard Penny saying, "No one would want to sail away with *that* weirdo. She'll be setting sail on her own."

Mayberry imagined jumping off the stage and smacking Penny . . . and the distraction made her voice crack. The piano trailed off.

She turned to Miss Speca, her cheeks growing hot. "Can I start over?"

"Fine," Miss Speca said without turning away from her music. She started playing the intro again.

"Okay . . ." Mayberry listened for her opening and began a second time, but she could see the girls laughing at her. This would never have happened in New York, where people did theater because they loved it, not because it racked up popularity points. Mayberry stumbled over the lyrics and froze in embarrassment. She sighed and dropped her head, trying to take the deep, calming breaths her mom's yoga teacher had recommended.

Her mouth was bone-dry, but she wanted to try one more time. "I can do this," she said to Miss Speca, in a low, quavering voice.

"Perhaps you can do it *someday*," Miss Speca said, her piano bench screeching as she pushed it away from the instrument. "But I've heard enough *for now*."

Mayberry scurried off the stage and ran down the aisle. "Loser," Penny hissed as Mayberry rushed by.

"Go back to where you came from, you weirdo," a petite blonde in a blue sweater set called out.

"Learn to sing," Kylie said, joining Penny and her pack of clones.

"Now, ladies, civility please!" Miss Speca said, even as she rolled her eyes at Mayberry's retreating figure.

They're right. I am a loser here. And a weirdo. This is pa-thetic, Mayberry thought.

Growing up in Manhattan, Mayberry had been schooled in its unique street ethos, where the ability to fence with words was an important survival skill. But she lacked the drive, much less inspiration, to defend herself here. Firing back clever retorts took wit and a deft touch, but here she felt dull and dispirited. All she wanted now was to go home, bake a batch of cookies, and eat them while watching some reality TV.

When Mayberry turned thirteen, her mother had told her that her teenage years would be an amazing time: she'd start sorting out who she was and what she wanted to do with her life. But instead of figuring things out, she was adrift in Eden Grove, becoming a portrait of apathy. A week ago she'd seen graffiti scribbled on a brick wall in an alley near Main Street that read YOU'RE NEVER TOO YOUNG TO DREAM BIG and realized that this optimistic aphorism didn't apply to her any-more. All her dreams stayed stuck to the pillow when she got up in the morning. Mayberry couldn't be herself in this town or learn the skills she would need later on as an adult. She needed to be somewhere . . . anywhere . . . else.

CHAPTER 3

MAYBERRY SPED PAST the row where Marshall was sitting as she scrambled out of the auditorium, angrily slamming her palm into the metal bar to flip open the exit door. Marshall darted out of his seat and followed.

"Mayberry," he called at her retreating back. She'd already made it past the classrooms and rows of industrial lockers, and was nearly at the front entrance.

She glanced over her shoulder and waved briefly. Not quite a greeting, but not a dismissal either.

"Want to talk about it?" he said as he walked up to her and held out his hands. For a second it seemed like he was going to put them on her shoulders to help calm her, but he stuffed them in his pockets instead.

She vigorously shook her head while staring into the

cracked concrete walkway—as if the secret to a happy life were scribbled on it somewhere in chalk. Then she turned toward home, nimbly dodging through the clumps of students standing by the school's front gate. They barely registered her presence . . . she could have been a veil of smoke they could see through.

Marshall paused and idly ran his hands over his hair, making it stick up even more. Then he reached into his pocket and whipped out his phone.

Those grls r losrs, he texted.

A few seconds later, her response pinged through. **TT,** she wrote. *True, true.*

He liberally interpreted her vague reply as an invitation to walk her home. With a few quick strides, he caught up. He let her occupy the weed-choked cracked sidewalk while he crunched through the fall leaves strewn in the road's gutter.

Her route home took them through the middle of Eden Grove's primary shopping area. It consisted of a few blocks of inelegant retail buildings bunched next to each other along both sides of their joke of a Main Street. Once considered quaint by visitors, the washed-out buildings had gone from antique to merely dilapidated. Most were faced with chipped, stained brick, some had cracked windows, and a few retained old-fashioned wooden signs that hung over creaky doors.

A new interstate highway had been built ten years ago, but it skirted the town's center by nearly fifteen miles. Eden Grove wasn't a convenient highway stop, and it had never developed a tourist attraction compelling enough to lure people off the road. Compounding the town's woes, its biggest employer, a Winnebago-type RV manufacturing plant, closed when gas prices rose and the economy tanked. Inexorably, the town's economy continued to wither and die. Kristi's Jewelry Store shuttered. H & T Bakery moved. Ace Hardware closed. And so on.

There wasn't much for teenagers to do in Eden Grove. A skating rink, a two-screen movie theater, and a rickety bowling alley made up their prime entertainment choices. Most of the young locals planned on leaving someday so they could live more stimulating lives elsewhere. Sadly, lethargy and fear often overcame their ambition, and few managed to escape.

Mayberry and Marshall watched as Mr. Hamner bounced out of his empty barbershop and idled on the sidewalk, trying to spot a male passerby who needed a haircut or shave but didn't realize it yet. The neatly trimmed Fu Manchu mustache perched below his bulbous nose showed off his barber skills, and his thick, ungainly body revealed the fact that he wasn't a man prone to dieting or exercise.

Looking straight at Mr. Hamner's jowly face, Marshall texted **Walrus** to Mayberry without missing a step.

Mayberry smirked.

As they approached the next corner, Mrs. Thomas, the bank manager's prissy wife, passed by. Her oversized oval sunglasses were parked on the bridge of her sharp nose, and her white hair was teased into a perfect bouffant. Neatly pressed khakis and a crisp blue shirt with an embroidered American flag on the front pocket completed her look.

Mayberry's fingers flashed back a text: **Poodle.**

Marshall laughed as he shuffled through the leaves.

A few blocks later, they turned off Main Street, and Mayberry stopped in the driveway of a rambling colonial-style home.

"See ya tomorrow," Marshall said, peering into Mayberry's face. "Unless maybe you want to hang out tonight?"

Mayberry shrugged, walked up the driveway, and passed through the house's front door without having uttered a single word since abandoning the auditorium stage.

CHAPTER 4

EONS BEFORE HE WAS BORN, Marshall's forebears had been the wealthiest and most prestigious family in the county. The Jackson Mansion was perched on top of Eden Grove's biggest hill, like a hungry vulture scouting for carrion.

A professional paintbrush hadn't touched its red clapboard siding in decades, and its steeply pitched roof was missing shingles, exposing weathered tarpaper underneath. The square tower attached to its roof was the highest point in town, from which an observer could see miles of surrounding countryside in every direction.

Marshall's late grandfather, James Jackson, had started the family's downward slide by investing in a variety of ill-considered ventures: mink farms, uranium mines in the Arctic Circle, oil exploration in the Baja desert, and other equally foolish get-rich-quick schemes. Finally, almost broke, he subdivided the virgin land around the mansion and chopped down the graceful old-growth pine trees that had blanketed it. Then he sold the lots to quick-buck developers who played off the proximity to the Jackson Mansion. This resulted in the worst kind of urban blight: a decaying old mansion surrounded by flimsy mini mansions packed together so tightly they nearly rubbed against each other.

Unfortunately, Marshall's parents had done nothing to improve the family finances. They continued James Jackson's downward spiral while living beneath a veneer of inherited dignity and the mantle of being the "Eden Grove Jacksons." For as long as they could, they'd supported their lavish lifestyle by auctioning off the mansion's art and antique furnishings, and now the house's interior looked like a looted museum.

Marshall walked up the cracked asphalt driveway that led to the mansion. He opened the faded green front door and immediately heard his parents' sharp-tongued bickering. *Nothing new there*, he thought.

"Things would be different," his mother croaked from the den, "if you would just get busy and—"

"Me get busy?" his father interrupted. "*Me?* I'm the one who . . ."

Marshall crept by the two ratty velveteen armchairs they occupied and slipped upstairs. How he'd managed to stay out of his family's muck was one of the great mysteries of

Darwinian evolution, like the way tiny, blind shrimp prospered miles below the ocean's surface, living in pitch-black water that circled hot volcanic vents.

Marshall's limited expertise with money extended primarily to squeaking by without much. Thankfully, he was a whiz with electronics and was able to pick up enough repair and programming work to keep himself equipped with new technology and a decent pair of sneakers. Still, his hard-earned cash would disappear if he left it anywhere his mother might find it. Neither of them spoke about the game of financial hide-and-seek they played, but he'd finally started winning when he stashed his paltry savings in an empty tuna can hidden in the very back of the pantry. His mother believed that her delicate palate was much too refined for tuna, which worked out well for Marshall.

Being a "Jackson" was a lifelong burden. Because Marshall's parents behaved as though they were inherently superior to the other townspeople, they were generally despised, and the locals passed down their feelings to their children, some of whom hated Marshall on principle. A handful of classmates, led by Marshall's longtime nemesis, Jim Campbell, had bullied him since grade school, solely because he was a Jackson. Fighting back only seemed to turn up the volume of their hostility, so Marshall had decided acceptance was his best option. This was the crummy state of affairs he'd grown accustomed to.

His loneliness and melancholy were like a wet wool blanket encasing his soul. Social networks? Not for him. He'd almost thrown up after he sampled what some of his classmates were posting about him online, so he never went back. He had a recurring nightmare in which he was trapped on a human hamster wheel, doomed to spend eternity living his high school years in Eden Grove over and over.

To keep his sanity intact, Marshall planned and executed clever pranks on his worst tormentors. For instance, he once broke into Jim's locker and altered his midterm take-home math quiz by replacing Jim's wrong answers with correct ones. Jim was terrible at math, and had been failing the course, so his teacher turned the dumbfounded fool in to the principal for cheating. He was suspended for a week.

Never experiencing even a modicum of a viable high school social life gave Marshall ample free time, which he mainly spent playing *World of Warcraft*. He was an Undead Warlock, and led a bloodthirsty band of followers in the Horde to dozens of victories against the Alliance. Other players respected and envied his avatar's leadership and fighting skills. Unfortunately, when Marshall passed through the school's main entrance, he shed the mantle of superhero and became an outcast.

CHAPTER 5

SOPHOMORE YEAR, a bright bolt of lightning had struck when Mayberry transferred to his school. She seemed to dislike the other students as much as they disliked him, and she stood out like a brightly plumed peacock in a flock of pigeons.

After discreetly watching her for a day or two, Marshall had finally introduced himself. Since she didn't reject his company, he'd hung around, asking questions about her life in New York City and giving her the rundown on the school's various characters. By the end of Mayberry's first week, he knew he'd finally found a kindred spirit. A glowing buoy of hope named Mayberry Hansen floated by his side, parting the choppy waters of his loneliness.

To him, Mayberry was the embodiment of the oddball cool kids he hung out with online. As they got to know each other, she introduced him to new and obscure music, and invited him over to watch somewhat bizarre nihilist movies. She even introduced him to wacky comics like Naruto and Tank Girl. He thought she was incredibly talented . . . and beautiful. His mindless classmates thought of her as just another off-center dork like him.

Even though Mayberry was the first girl he'd ever really spent quality time with—and certainly the prettiest—she became his closest friend. It wasn't long before he was always thinking about her. As the weeks passed, his attraction grew, getting harder and harder for him to conceal. His palms started to sweat and he felt a strangely unnerving pleasure in her presence. Even when they weren't together, images of her were always popping into his mind. He'd never seriously considered having a girlfriend before, and knew telling Mayberry how he felt might ruin their friendship, but he couldn't help wondering if she could ever see him as more than just a friend. For now, he'd decided it was safer to accept their friendship the way it was rather than risking losing it.

CHAPTER 6

MAYBERRY BURST through the front door and dumped her black patent-leather backpack on the floor.

"I'm home," she called out to the flowers that sat on the foyer's end table. She pulled off her jacket and kicked off her shoes, then headed for the living room.

Her mom was out in the field doing research. Her dad was sitting on the couch with his laptop propped up on some pillows. He pulled his legs down and patted the seat next to him.

"Hi, kiddo," he said. "How'd your audition go?"

She shook her head, refusing his invitation. "An absolute joy, from start to finish," she said. "You can't even imagine."

He raised his eyebrows and wrinkled his nose. "Does that mean you got a part?"

"I got what I deserved," she said with finality.

Life was always throwing her curveballs she couldn't identify or hit. She certainly wasn't batting home runs at school, and she was no domestic goddess, either. Her mom once joked that Mayberry risked burning down the house just trying to make toast. Nonetheless, she headed toward the kitchen. Chocolate chip cookies were her one and only specialty. Measuring, mixing, stirring, and rolling the tasty dough into neat circles gave her great satisfaction. Breathing deeply as the kitchen filled with the sweet aroma of cookies baking never failed to set her mind at ease. Plus, after only eight minutes in the oven, voilà! She had delicious cookies to eat, filled with extra helpings of chocolate.

It was a win-win.

CHAPTER 7

MAYBERRY MUNCHED a fresh cookie while poring over the full-color satellite map that was pasted on the wall of her mother's office.

More than four feet wide by three feet tall, the map's detailed photographs covered over a hundred fifty square miles of the area's forests. The map was marked by numbered red dots that identified the sites her mother still wanted to explore, and an army of blue dots confirmed the ones she'd already visited. Most of the blue dots pinpointed locations that were miles away from Eden Grove, while the red dots represented the local forests she hadn't visited yet.

Mayberry had a knack for operating complex instruments that surpassed her mom's talents, so she'd volunteered to act as her mom's tech guru. This, coupled with her love for and understanding of science, made her a brilliant—and free—assistant.

Marshall texted Mayberry: **:/ You okay? Feel like company?**

Sure, she texted back. **Come on over.**

The sheer tonnage of gear crammed into the workspace was enough to make a hoarder cry. There were no fewer than three high-speed computers, an electron microscope, a gas chromatograph, a mass spectrometer, and scores of more complicated equipment that would have been foreign to even a knowledgeable tech geek. Her mom's pride and joy was a leased epifluorescence microscope that could identify and record the reflected glow of a single molecule. Stacked cardboard boxes of spiral notebooks filled with her mother's scribbled notes crowded one corner of the room.

Line after line of photos of individual aspen trees and groves were tacked to the walls and marked with numbered blue dots that corresponded to the dots on the satellite map. Also clipped to the individual tree photos were greatly magnified images of the cross sections of core samples taken by her mother and matched with the results of a DNA analytic program. The dozens of small metal specimen containers that held the core samples were stacked in the corner, numbered to match the appropriate blue dots.

Mayberry cut careful cross sections from some untested core samples, took microscopic pictures, and methodically cataloged the photos. When her mom had time after all the data was obtained, she'd determine whether the aspens in this part of the country were healthy or diseased like so many of the aspen forests in the west.

There was a rap on the front door, then the sound of her father answering. After some low murmurs, she heard someone clomping upstairs toward the office. Marshall stuck his head through the doorway and waited for her to wave him in. After she did, he grinned and strolled into the room. He knew her mom was a scientist, but had never seen the office before, and his eyes opened wider as he appraised the room's contents.

"What's up with all this?" he asked, walking around in circles and clasping his hands together, as if to keep them from reaching out and touching the instruments. "And what are *you* doing with it?"

Mayberry pulled off her white latex gloves and sat in the desk chair. "My mom's studying local aspen trees to see how the recent changes in climate patterns have affected their health."

"Sounds interesting," he said, looking at the dots on the satellite map and then the tree photos.

"It's pretty cool. She's lucky I like science." Mayberry glanced up at Marshall from under her long lashes, and her lips twisted into a barely discernable smirk. "Proving the effects of climate change is the priority, but she hopes to find the world's biggest quaking aspen colony while she's at it."

"What?"

"I'll explain. The most massive and maybe the oldest single

organism on Earth is a quaking aspen colony that lives on the shores of Fish Lake in south-central Utah. It covers more than a hundred and six acres, and weighs more than thirteen million pounds. If my mom can find a bigger aspen grove that's a single colony—meaning all part of one tree—she'll be famous."

"That's cool," he said, crossing his arms and pulling his wool sweater off over his head. "But aren't redwoods the oldest trees?"

"Not even," she said. "There are two really old trees in the Sierra Nevada Mountains—a giant sequoia that's two hundred forty-seven feet high and at least three thousand two hundred years old, and a bristlecone pine that's more than four thousand seven hundred years old. But biologists think some quaking aspen colonies may be over eighty thousand years old."

"Seriously? How do they get so old? And big?" Marshall said.

"They're big because the individual aspens you see above ground are actually offshoots of one tree bound together by a giant root system. They're old because even when some of the grove's individual trees or roots wither and die, they're replaced by clones that are part of the larger underground organism, and they keep dying and being reborn again and again.

"It's a ton of extra work for my mom, though, because you can't tell if it's a quaking aspen colony by checking the DNA of just one piece of wood—you have to take samples encompassing the whole grove. If Mom actually finds a big grove, I'll use the instruments in this room to figure out its age."

Marshall ran a hand through his hair. "Wow. I knew you were into science, but I had no idea you were *this* into science."

Mayberry blushed and shrugged.

CHAPTER 8

MARSHALL STROLLED BACK to the satellite map and pressed his index finger into a relatively big red-dotted aspen grove. "That's the aspen grove the town council likes to call the Mystery Forest," he said, looking down at Mayberry, who was standing beside him now. "It's just outside of town."

Mayberry's hands involuntarily shot out and grabbed Marshall's wrists. "*What?*"

"Consider yourself lucky that you haven't heard the stupid stories about it millions of times." He looked down at his wrists, smiling, and Mayberry let go. "The town council invented myths about it to attract tourists to the forest, but too many people got lost, so you need a permit to get in now. Basically, it's just a really big aspen grove in the middle of a pine forest."

"Weird," she said, frowning.

"Exactly. The coolest myth they invented is about a tree that lives at the exact center of the forest. If you find it, and ask the right way, the tree will grant your wish. Now that we're talking about it, it seems like I should have found it years ago and wished for a new life, ha-ha."

"That's awesome. A Wishing Tree. Tell me more."

He pursed his lips, thinking. "Okay, one hiker disappeared and was never found. Not even a trace. And one dude who did get back—he'd had dark hair and it turned white in the forest, and he went completely nuts in there. And when I was in eighth grade, this kid in the class a year behind me went in and they eventually found him there in a *coma*."

"Whoa. That's strange," she exclaimed. "There's got to be some kind of explanation for the myth. Maybe one tree is creepier looking than the rest of them, or just bigger. Forget the permits. Let's go look for the magic tree this weekend. My parents are going to New York for work on Friday night. They won't be back until next Thursday. Anyway, it'll be fun for me because I've never hiked through a real forest."

Mayberry twirled winningly, and Marshall laughed.

"If you want," he said, a dubious expression on his face. He was no outdoorsman, but he couldn't say no to Mayberry. Maybe his technology could save him.

CHAPTER 9

MARSHALL GOT UP EARLY on Saturday morning. He was excited about hanging out with Mayberry, but felt a general sense of anxiety about the trip. If they were caught in the restricted area, the Forest Service could fine each of them a thousand dollars, and he didn't *have* a thousand dollars. He tried to channel his energy into preparing for the trip, throwing water and snacks in a backpack and finding the fancy GPS unit he'd got in exchange for helping some guy with his server.

At around eight A.M., Mayberry texted, telling him she was waiting outside. He pulled on his backpack and shuffled downstairs.

Mayberry was leaning on her pristine red mountain bike's handlebars, waiting for him to mount his own dinged and dented green bike. She smiled and raised her eyebrows. "You ready, Marshall?"

"Sure," he said halfheartedly.

"We don't *have* to do this," she said, picking up his dour mood.

Marshall responded by gearing up and pedaling toward the forest.

Mayberry had abandoned her usual school uniform of baggy blacks for a colorful hiking outfit: tight jeans and a snug yellow pullover, topped by a loose red puffer vest. Even though she was dressed fairly simply, she wasn't trying to hide her body. The overall impact was—well—really great. Marshall's heart beat harder as he looked at her. *Don't go there,* he warned himself. So far their relationship had been totally cloudless, and he didn't want to risk screwing that up.

"What's up?" she asked, pulling her bike up beside his.

"Nothing," he replied, waving vaguely at the scenery. "It's just . . . really pretty here."

"This is going to be amazing," she said, reaching out a finger to ding her bike's bell.

In another mile, they pulled onto the shoulder of the narrow dirt road to let a beat-up Chevy pickup rattle past. Soon after that they rode into a lot that was marked MYSTERY FOREST PARKING. It was crisp and sunny out, but the only vehicle there was a battered green jeep with a peeling Forest Service sticker on its door.

They dismounted and slid their bikes under some bushes at the edge of the lot, just in case.

CHAPTER 10

A STRAIGHT-BACKED, wooden slat bench sat in the shade cast by the dilapidated log cabin overlooking the meadow. The park ranger was sprawled across it, snoring like a sawmill, and wearing a uniform he must have acquired sixty pounds ago. A paperback novel titled *Shauna's Romance* was open and resting on his gut. Gracing the book's cover was a heavily muscled man with long, blond rock-star hair, embracing a scantily clad woman.

It would be laughably easy for Mayberry and Marshall to slip past him and head into the forest.

"I can hardly wait to get in there," she whispered to Marshall, reaching out to squeeze his arm. She felt like a city girl on her first field trip to the country.

"Me too," Marshall responded, a little lightheaded from her touch. This time he actually meant it.

She read some of the signs facing the parking lot as she stretched the kinks out of her back. One noted that the Sioux Indians considered the Mystery Forest to be a sacred place from which their medicine man's spirit could journey to another world. Another claimed that a special tree inside granted wishes to those with a noble heart. She had every intention of finding that giant aspen and trying it out, but as far as she was concerned, science always ruled. The real world was a bizarre enough place without bringing supernatural claptrap into it. She smiled gleefully when she noticed the two yellow NO TRESPASSING signs posted by the ends of the fence. Forbidden Territory loomed ahead.

Mayberry and Marshall climbed the fence, startling a herd of grazing mule deer. Marshall's face broke out in a smile, and he shrugged as the deer darted away. After a short trek across the meadow, they reached a covered wooden bridge that spanned a narrow river. Leaves and other debris floated in the gentle current, and something splashed into the water as they stepped onto the bridge's creaky timbers.

Mayberry paused for a second to admire the stand of pines in the forest they were about to enter, then moved forward, zipping her vest tighter as she crossed into the shade of the trees. The temperature difference was vast—it was if someone had whipped off her blanket on a cold winter's night.

"Let's go that way," Marshall said, pointing to a trail. He placed his palm in the small of Mayberry's back and pushed her forward gently, and the two started up the trail at an admirable clip. Accustomed to exercising only her brain and typing fingers, beads of sweat soon broke on Mayberry's forehead, and her leg muscles burned as they picked their way through the forest. The faint buzzing sounds of mosquitoes reminded her that she should have brought insect repellent.

After ten minutes of walking, Mayberry leaned down and put her hands on her knees. "Can we . . . take a . . . break?" she panted. "Just for . . . a minute . . ."

Marshall nodded and shrugged off his backpack, then sat down, leaning against the trunk of one of the pines. He rummaged in his pack, then withdrew a canteen, which he offered to Mayberry.

Mayberry unscrewed the silver cap and took a few deep gulps. "That's better," she said, handing it back to Marshall.

He rested his head against the tree, enjoying the moment. He wasn't that accomplished of an outdoorsman, but at least he'd packed well enough to make himself seem a *little* experienced.

He took a swig from the canteen and rose, then extended a hand to Mayberry. "Ready?"

She grabbed his hand and allowed him to haul her up, then held out both arms and arched her back. "Ready."

CHAPTER 11

FOR A WHILE all the trees they hiked through were evergreens. It seemed like an eternity before they crossed into the aspen grove. There, the tree trunks were tall, slender, and as graceful as the legs of a thousand ballerinas. The leaves were every shade of yellow and gold, and the slightest breeze set them flashing in the sunlight. They stretched for acres and acres, without any other tree species mixed in. Mayberry had seen groves of aspens changing color during road trips with her parents along the coastline of New England, but the sight of so many bunched close together was breathtaking. Trespassing or no, she couldn't wait to tell her mother.

Marshall looked around. "So this is it. The famous Mystery Forest. I can't believe I've never been here before. These aspen trees are cool, but I thought once we got here they would be . . . I don't know, spookier or something. Are these the quaking kind?"

She peered carefully at the trees around them. They *might* be quaking aspens. "We'll take some samples, and I'll check them when I get home. Break off little branches here and there, and stick them in your backpack."

"No problem. I don't even have to break them," he said pulling off his backpack. He swung it around, dug into the front pocket, and flashed a Swiss Army knife, then flicked out its serrated blade.

Her mom believed that breaking or cutting branches was a huge no-no. To ensure she didn't harm the trees, she used a sterilized micro core-borer to take samples. Mayberry would eventually have to come up with a rational explanation for how she happened to get the samples from the protected forest, but that was tomorrow's problem.

"Let's keep going," Mayberry said, acknowledging the knife with a conspiratorial smile. "We didn't see the Wishing Tree on my mom's satellite maps. So how do we find the center of the forest?"

"We use this," Marshall said, pulling the GPS unit from the backpack and pressing a green button on its side. While it booted up, he passed her a crinkled bag of M&M's.

"With a grove this dense, it's easy to get lost. This GPS unit is the best in its class—even better since I modified it last night. It's got super-fast satellite acquisition, a screen you can read in daylight or pitch-darkness, three hundred thousand preprogrammed waypoints, and batteries that last for two weeks. I downloaded the satellite photo from Google Earth and laid an electronic grid over it, so it should be able to plot the fastest route to the center waypoint. All we have to do is follow the path it calculates. Simple."

"That's amazing," she said, shaking her head in wonder and a bit taken aback that he had gone to all that trouble for her. Whether they found the tree or not, this trip was turning out better than she'd expected.

"Look, if we get lost using this, I'll . . . well, I don't know. I'll eat a caterpillar. Or whatever kind of bug we can find."

"If we get lost while using that thing, I'll be too busy laughing to watch you eat the caterpillar."

"Trust me," he said with a Cheshire cat grin. "Just trust me."

Seconds after he turned it on, the GPS's screen started scrolling through random maps, its waypoints indicating they were in Siberia, then the Gobi Desert, then Ashland, Kansas. Finally it let out a defeated whine and powered itself off.

Marshall's eyes bulged while Mayberry shrieked with laughter.

"I can't believe it," he said. "This was working *perfectly* last night."

He checked the batteries, then rebooted the unit. The machine hummed as it turned on, then began flipping through maps again.

"Marshall, you should shut that thing off before it gives us seizures," Mayberry said with a smirk.

With a final shake of his head, Marshall removed the battery pack, closed the cover, and stuffed the device into his backpack. He pulled his blue baseball cap off with one hand and scratched the back of his head with the other. Then he whipped out his cell phone. The screen flashed, then went dark. The same thing happened when Mayberry tried hers.

"It's like we're in a technological black hole," Marshall said. "Finding out why should be your mother's research project."

Mayberry laughed. "No kidding. In the meantime, I'll start looking for your caterpillar. The M&M's can be just for me."

"Hilarious." He tilted his head back and looked up at the pine trees, and the cool blue sky peeking around them.

"Let's start walking," Mayberry said. "If we keep the sun at our backs, we'll find the center eventually. This grove can't be *that* big."

CHAPTER 12

TIME SEEMED TO SLOW while they walked through the aspen grove. After ten or fifteen yards, the trees formed an impenetrable wall that seemed to go on forever. No wonder casual hikers weren't allowed in.

After a while, the aspens' trunks were bunched so close that their branches interlaced overhead in a tangled mass that shut out more and more sunlight. It had become impossible to tell which way they were going. The trunks were getting thicker too, and more gnarled. Did some of the folds, knots, and markings on them vaguely resemble grimacing faces? No. Of course not.

Mayberry thought some of the branches seemed to be waving at her in the wind, greeting her like they did in the fairy tales about magic forests she'd read as a child.

Marshall, who was walking a few feet to her left, pointed to the ground. "Check this out. I think it's another trail."

Whether humans or animals had scraped this faint path, Mayberry couldn't tell, but it wound conveniently through the underbrush.

Moments later, something in her gut confirmed that they were getting closer to the center. She couldn't explain why, but she just knew.

And then they were there. Facing them was an open clearing covered with leaves, with one humongous tree anchoring its center. Mayberry had seen pictures of ancient redwoods and giant sequoias, and this tree seemed to have as much or more girth but possibly less height. But its total mass, with all the giant limbs blasting skyward, seemed to be even bigger. She couldn't even see its top through all the limbs and branches, so it appeared to stretch to the moon or the sun or beyond.

Marshall craned his neck, looking up, "Wow, look at the size of *that* mother."

Wild giggles bubbled from Mayberry, and soon, both of them were doubled over, clutching their sides, their laughter way out of proportion to his comment.

"That . . ." she said, addressing the tree as she struggled to catch her breath, "that really is a *big mother*, isn't it? It's weird that we didn't see it while we were walking this way."

They sat down under the shade of the giant tree. Mayberry couldn't stop thinking about how there was something unique about this aspen, standing alone like—well, as Marshall said, a mother, a matriarch, surrounded by a clan of worshipful offspring who stayed at a respectful distance. Mayberry got up and strolled toward its trunk, reaching out to touch the smooth bark. Despite the chilly autumn air, an inexplicable warmth pulsed through her fingertips and deep into the rest of her body. She'd have sworn she could feel a faint beat under its bark. She watched Marshall walk up and place his hands next to hers on the trunk. His jaw dropped in wonder.

"What now?" Marshall asked in a low voice. "If there is a Wishing Tree, this is it." He looked at Mayberry appraisingly. "Are we going to make a wish? Should we make one together?"

"Absolutely. But I have to warn you, wishes don't usually come true for me," she said, scooting away and flipping onto her back so that her head nestled in the base of the trunk. She stretched out her hands behind her and ran her fingers along the bark. Over her head, its branches bobbed and weaved in the breeze.

Marshall snickered, then mirrored her position, resting his head close to hers. "They never come true for me either. But we're here, so we have to do it."

Mayberry turned to him. His brown eyes had little flecks of amber that she'd never noticed before. She ducked her head back down.

"So what do you want to wish for?"

"I don't know," he said pensively. "A lot of money, I guess."

Mayberry looked at the branches above her and sighed.

"Money is useful, and I get why you want it, but it definitely doesn't make you happy. Your family used to have a lot of it, and your life isn't so great right now because of it, you know? Anything else you can think of?"

"Maybe we should ask to go on an amazing voyage," Marshall said with a laugh. "Like a *Star Trek* trip: we could go to an alien world, but a world where humans can live without space suits."

"Ha! That would be awesome," Mayberry said. "Okay, I've got one. Everything you asked for, plus we can do magic."

"Magic?" Marshall said, turning to give her a quizzical look.

"Sure," Mayberry said, fiddling with the zipper on her vest. "Like Harry Potter."

"Fine," he said, grinning. "We can use our magic to help people and be, like, superheroes. Okay, close your eyes and focus on our wish."

Mayberry closed her eyes, then reached out and clasped Marshall's hand.

Mayberry focused and focused, and it turned out that thinking about her wishes was sort of like meditating. It was still early in the morning, but she started drifting off to sleep. Her hand released Marshall's and dropped to the forest floor. She half opened her eyes and saw that Marshall was already asleep. The last thing she glimpsed, as her eyelids closed, was a cascade of leaves whirling down from the tree, like handfuls of golden feathers.

CHAPTER 13

MAYBERRY GRADUALLY WOKE UP and opened her eyes. Marshall was still sleeping beside her. She groaned a little and rolled awkwardly to her knees, then used her hands to push against the Wishing Tree's trunk and get to her feet. Marshall, sensing her movement, blinked and rose up on his elbows. The shape of an aspen leaf was imprinted in dirt on his right cheek.

"We fell asleep," she said, stating the obvious, then tilting her head to look up at the Tree.

"Yeah we did. Let's go. I don't know how long we slept, and we don't want to be caught in here after dark." He took a step, then stopped. "Wait a minute. Is it *hot*?"

"It *is* hot," she said, eyes widening. "Sort of humid, too."

He turned in a slow circle. "I think we came from that

way," he said, pointing to a patch of aspens that looked exactly like every other patch. "Maybe."

She peered in the direction he'd pointed, trying to spot the trail or anything familiar. "This is crazy. I really wish your GPS worked."

Marshall nodded. "Let's just go. We know we're in the center of the grove, so any direction will take us out of the forest eventually, and then we can circle around to the bikes."

She started walking into the aspens, and he fell in step behind her.

After a short while, they exited the grove, but instead of coming to the border of evergreens, they emerged at the edge of a field of tall green grass. It was chest-high on Marshall and nearly reached Mayberry's chin.

The air was much warmer—it felt almost like summer. Plus she felt . . . lighter now, as though moving her limbs took less effort. The dense grass smelled like cloves and moss mixed with tart lemon.

Mayberry paused while Marshall tried his GPS again, and then his phone. Neither device worked. Mayberry started thinking about all those lost hikers. Where had they ended up?

Marshall finally spoke. "Look, something is really wrong. It's way too hot for an autumn day, and I have *never* seen grass this tall anywhere in Minnesota."

"Chill, Marshall," Mayberry said. "The temperature swing isn't *that* crazy, and this field is probably buffalo grass. It used to cover the whole Midwest, and settlers talked about how it grew as high as a horse's belly. The Forest Service must be preserving this patch, which is probably the real reason you need a permit."

She could tell by the look on Marshall's face that he wasn't buying her answer, but she didn't care. Negativity wasn't going to get them back to the bikes. She plunged into the grass, and they waded through it together.

"If we keep the aspen grove on our right, we've got to find the other meadow sooner or later," she said confidently.

"I guess," Marshall said, frowning and hitching up his jeans.

They'd been walking for a few more minutes when he grabbed her arm. "Hey, did it rain while we were sleeping?"

Mayberry quirked her mouth and rolled her eyes a little. "I doubt it. We're not wet, and neither is the ground. Why?"

"Because there's a rainbow," he said, pointing up at the sky.

Marshall was right. Brilliant ribbons of color arched across the clear blue sky. Something was off about it, though. Mayberry stared for a minute, then realized that the colors weren't layered in the right positions. She looked down at the grass, then back up again. Now it seemed like the colors had shifted.

"It's gorgeous," she said. "But strange. Are the colors changing?"

Marshall and Mayberry kept their eyes on the rainbow, which was clearly moving now, coming toward them, floating across the sky like a Chinese dragon kite, coming closer and closer until it was right over their heads. Shocked, Mayberry grasped Marshall's shoulder just as the rainbow burst like a supernova, breaking into thousands of smaller pieces that formed a V shape and sped away. They gaped in astonishment.

"They're *birds*," she cried gleefully. "I can't believe that just happened. Where the hell *are* we?" She breathed hard and turned to Marshall. "Do you think it worked? Our wish?"

Marshall squeezed his eyes tight for a second, and when he opened them, Mayberry was still there, and they were still in the meadow, and delicate bits of rainbow-colored plumage floated down on their heads and shoulders.

"Maybe. Or we're still dreaming. Let's just keep trying to find a way back to the bikes."

"Oh my God, look at this," Mayberry said, pushing through the grass toward a foot-long feather, delicate as gossamer, clinging to a blade of grass. Its colors were as iridescent as those on a butterfly wing; the green of fresh mint, the aqua of the Caribbean sea, the dark blue of the sky just before sunset, and more—all in something barely twice as long as her hand. She plucked it from the grass, turning it over in her fingers. A burst of pleasant electric energy jolted her.

"Aah," she gasped involuntarily.

"What?"

"Nothing bad. I touched a feather, and it gave me a little tingly shock." She handed the feather over to Marshall as power prickled through her. She was energized—so energized she felt like she *had* to move. She leaped away and started running straight into the grassy meadow.

"Mayberry!" Marshall yelled at her retreating back. "What are you doing? Stop."

"I'm just *going*," she shouted back over her shoulder.

Overflowing with energy, Mayberry was able to run faster and jump higher than she ever had before. Her sneakers drummed the hard-packed earth as she tore through the thick grass that had slowed her passage just moments before. She heard Marshall's voice in the background shouting for her to stop, but her pace left him farther and farther behind, and everything around her was a blur. Then she heard him racing up behind her with his long legs scissoring rapidly through the grass, moving even faster than she was. When he finally caught up, he tapped her lightly on the shoulder with the feather and smiled as he raced by.

She dug deep and came back with a burst of speed, getting close enough to return Marshall's tap. They sprinted side by side for a few more yards. When they finally tumbled onto the grass, they were both panting, which soon turned into giddy laughter that made their sides ache.

This was becoming one of Mayberry's favorite days ever.

CHAPTER 14

AFTER CATCHING HIS BREATH, Marshall looked around and tried to get his bearings. The aspen grove was now *way* behind them; their energetic run had carried them farther than he'd have thought possible. Thankfully, he could still make out the faint flash of gold leaves in the distance.

"All right," he said, reaching out to tug down the zipper on Mayberry's winter vest. "We should keep heading in this direction—the plan is still to double back to the bikes, right?" Now that the adrenaline rush was fading, he had an uneasy feeling that they were in danger, and the hairs on the back of his neck prickled.

"Right," Mayberry agreed. As they started getting up, a soft chuffing sound came from somewhere near them. She jumped back. "What was *that*?"

The last thing she glimpsed was a cascade of leaves
whirling down from the tree, like handfuls of golden feathers.

"I don't know," he said, swallowing an equal mixture of surprise and concern. "Maybe a deer or something? There are bears in these woods, too."

The chuffing sounded again, followed by a sound that was similar, but with a higher pitch. There were more than one of whatever was out there.

"Let's look," said Mayberry.

"We should just get out of here," Marshall said, lifting his cap. "They could be dangerous."

"We'll be careful," she said, tugging gently on his sleeve. "Come on. We're *here*, right? Even if we don't exactly know what that means yet."

Marshall shook his head, but nodded toward the noise. They both started moving at a snail's pace in that direction, trying to keep from rustling the tall grass. In a few minutes, he glimpsed the upper bodies of a trio of animals that were vaguely horse shaped, but with camel humps and shaggy greenish fur marked with wide black stripes. Their heads were low to the ground at first—presumably they were eating grass—but then a furry green head popped up and gazed at them with huge, soulful yellow eyes.

"That's the craziest thing I've ever seen. Back away before it sees us," she whispered.

"Too late." The impossible *Alice in Wonderland* look of the thing was mesmerizing. "It definitely sees us."

Two other heads lifted, and now all three creatures were sizing them up. There was nothing malevolent in their stance or appearance, but the animals were bigger than horses, with long, powerful-looking necks like giraffes but thicker, and looked more powerful. The nearest creature swallowed a mouthful of grass and took a step toward them. It seemed to be either grinning or passing gas—Marshall couldn't tell for sure.

"Marshall . . ."

"I think it's just curious," he said, trying hard to keep calm. He backed up a step, and the nearest creature gave another soft chuff.

"Don't startle it," whispered Mayberry.

"Shhh." Marshall held his ground as the creature shambled closer. It stopped a few feet in front of them, close enough for him to smell its earthy breath.

A second one trotted up and stopped in front of Mayberry. Then both animals knelt down, lowering their heads and shoulders. For a second, Marshall thought the animals were bending to graze, but they kept their mouths closed and their eyes trained on the humans.

"They . . ." she began. He saw her swallow hard. "I think they want us to climb onto them."

"What?" No way. This wouldn't even happen on *Star Trek*. He took another step back as the creatures strained their heads forward, rolling their massive shoulders down below the level of the grass.

"Whatever they are, they're definitely friendly." Mayberry reached a hand tentatively toward the kneeling beast, patting the fur on the back of its neck. Getting bolder, she scratched it gently between its hairy green ears. It wrinkled the skin on the top of its head and chortled with delight.

"Marshall, I really think they want us to get on. This is a once-in-a-lifetime thing. We have to do it."

As Marshall stood frozen with indecision, she approached the kneeling beast. "Nice . . . thingie," she said soothingly. "Good thingie. Here goes nothing," she said, lifting her right foot over the animal's neck to straddle it and using its coarse hair to pull herself the rest of the way up.

The creature slowly rose to its feet. She slid backward until she stopped in a natural saddle, just behind where its neck joined its chest. When it reached its full height, Mayberry's feet dangled six feet above the ground. A wide grin covered her face, like a kid on the first day of summer vacation.

"Marshall," she cried, "this is unbelievable. You've got to do it!"

The other creature was still staring at him with those golden eyes as he gently pulled himself onto its neck. The beast raised its head slowly, and Marshall slid down and started to laugh. "I can't believe this."

"I know," said Mayberry, running her fingers through her creature's green pelt. "I know."

His creature took a couple of halting steps, and Marshall swayed unsteadily, grabbing the thick fur on its neck to stabilize him. "What do you want to—" But before he could spit out his question, both creatures shot off, galloping across the vast grassy meadow . . . and even farther away from the aspen forest.

The two animals tore swiftly along, side by side. Fortunately, the beast's natural saddle cradled him, and its rhythmic gallop made it surprisingly easy to stay aboard. The wind slapped Marshall's face, the sun glanced off the beasts' fur, and he heard the thunder of their hooves.

Flocks of dark blue creatures with two sets of parallel wings darted through the cloudless sky. After a few minutes, the practical side of Marshall's brain jerked to its senses as he realized that he had absolutely no idea where their mounts were taking them. He whipped his head around and saw that the aspens were no longer visible, only endless grass.

"Mayberry, we have to *stop*," he yelled across the gap between them. "We don't know where we're going."

Mayberry frowned. "You're right. *But how?*"

Marshall hadn't considered that question. "*Whoa!*" he shouted, as loudly as he could. When that didn't work, he grabbed the fur on both sides of the creature's neck and tugged. The creature slowed, then skidded to a jerky halt. Marshall almost flipped forward over its neck, barely managing to regain his balance. He awkwardly slid off of its back.

"Thanks for the ride, buddy," he said, gently patting the creature's head while backing away slowly.

Mayberry's beast turned around and trotted back to the one that had carried Marshall. Grasping its thick fur, she slid smoothly off. On foot again, they were wobbly-legged but unharmed.

The friendly beasts snorted, then barreled away.

"That was the most fun I've had in my whole life," Mayberry exclaimed with twinkling eyes and a huge smile. "What were those creatures? Where *are* we?"

"I know it's amazing, but honestly, I think we need to get back to the Mystery Forest," he said, pointedly ignoring her question as he tried to figure out the best way back based on the position of the sun. "I think we came north," he said. "Or . . . but . . . oh, I really don't know."

"Wherever we are, it feels pretty late." She glanced at her wrist and frowned. "My watch stopped," she said, raising her wrist to show him.

He checked his own watch. It had stopped at nine thirty A.M., about the time they'd fallen asleep by the tree.

She pointed toward a low hill—the highest point in the grassy countryside surrounding them. "Let's climb up and see if we can figure it out."

Marshall nodded and checked his belt where he'd tucked the feather Mayberry had found, but it was gone. Climbing the slope to the top of the hill was a slog. Once on its peak, he scrambled up onto a couple of huge quartz-like boulders.

It might not look familiar, but the landscape was undeniably beautiful. Jagged mountains in the far distance, shrouded in ominous gray and black clouds, framed the rolling grasslands. In the other direction was a dense forest with a towering canopy of leaves. Below their vantage point on the far left was a swiftly running river that sparkled with rolling white rapids.

Another revelation hit Marshall, like a copper nail driven into the center of his forehead. He'd never seen mountains like those anywhere near Eden Grove. The accumulating evidence was pretty convincing. Had the Wishing Tree actually transported them to another world?

As if Mayberry was reading his mind, she blurted out, "There has to be another explanation."

"Yeah. Right," he replied. "Exotic jungle birds with feathers that fall from the sky and speed you up when you touch them. New mountains. Not to mention those alien animals we rode."

She glanced down, her anxiety evident in her tremulous voice. "I don't care what the explanation is, Marshall. We *have* to find our way back home. Let's retrace our steps."

He nodded and shoved his hands deep into his pockets so Mayberry couldn't see that they were trembling.

CHAPTER 15

THEY HAD GONE a little farther when Mayberry sighed in relief.

"What?" said Marshall.

"Cows," she said, pointing to animals grazing in the distance. "There must be a farmhouse nearby, which means a working landline so we can get some help."

Marshall couldn't help but feel a tad disappointed by seeing such an ordinary animal. Now the only new adventure left for him to share with Mayberry would be finding a farmhouse on the cattle ranch. As they approached the river, he noticed how much broader it looked and how much faster it seemed to be running than when they'd crossed it on the covered wooden bridge.

Mayberry started walking faster, obviously excited, but she slowed as they drew closer. One of the animals turned sideways. The wide-bellied creature had a thick coat of curly brown fur, but it definitely wasn't a cow. Two sets of sharp, heavily ringed horns sprouted from its head, and a ridge of long jagged teeth lined a deep mouth.

It swung its massive head down to pull up some of the heavy grass growing near the river. The rest of the herd lingered nearby. Mayberry was disconcerted by the strange-looking beast, but even more worried by what seeing it meant. Sensing their presence, the beast whirled its head and regarded them with small, malevolent eyes. It stomped the earth with its front hooves a couple of times, like an angry bull warning a matador to back off. A low keening came from its mouth.

Then it charged.

"*Run!*" Marshall yelled.

Mayberry spun and ran as fast as she could, desperately wishing she had a feather to give her feet wings. The huge beast thundered after them, the ground quaking under the weight of its hooves. Too soon she heard a deep, ugly grunt behind her.

"*That way!*" she screamed, pointing right. Marshall obeyed, veering sharply, while Mayberry dodged hard to the left.

The charging beast leaned its head right, then left as its tiny brain tried to determine which of them to crush first. Confused, it dashed straight between them. A couple of dozen feet later, it planted its front legs in the grass and skidded to an unsteady halt, its hooves plowing deep grooves in the earth.

"*The river!*" Marshall bellowed, pivoting to sprint in the opposite direction.

Mayberry instantly understood Marshall's thinking. The beast was bulky, with relatively spindly legs—it probably couldn't swim. She dashed toward the water, straining to get every bit of horsepower out of her legs, but soon heard the crunching sound of the beast's hooves behind her. A painful stitch scorched her left side as her muscles started to cramp. She imagined the thing's breath on her neck—*gasp*—its deadly pointed horns slamming into her back—*gasp*—turning her vulnerable internal organs to jelly—*gasp*. Could she get to the river before the creature impaled her? She didn't have to find out, because Marshall had stopped ahead, waiting for her in front of a big, dead, tall moss-covered tree by the riverbank. His fingers were interlaced at thigh level to make a step for her foot.

"*Jump!*" he screamed.

Without thinking, she vaulted in full stride, planting her right foot squarely in the palms of his hands. He pushed her foot into the air, high enough for her to grab a branch with both hands. She shimmied rapidly up the tree and swung her legs over a thick branch.

Marshall jumped and deftly grabbed a low branch on the opposite side of hers, then scrambled up toward Mayberry's side of the tree just as the beast's horns rammed into the trunk beneath them. The tree vibrated to its core. The beast gnashed its teeth and looked up as the two climbed farther out of its reach. It reared back on its hind legs and squatted so low its flat tail almost touched the ground. Its legs compressed downward like metal springs. Then it jumped, propelling itself almost high enough to gash Mayberry's leg with one of its horns. While descending, the furious creature opened its maw and tore off a strip of bark, rather than the flesh it sought. Then, landing nimbly like a cat on all fours, it spat out the wad of bark and trotted away.

Marshall shot Mayberry a thumbs-up from a branch across from hers and started speaking, but the roar of the river crashing and churning below the tree muffled his words.

He tried again. "That was close," he yelled.

"Yeah. *Too* close," Mayberry shouted back.

She squinted down into the whitecaps swirling below. A hundred yards away was a wide waterfall with a ten-foot drop. A series of smaller waterfalls cascaded downriver from there, until the water finally mushed together into a narrow, fast-moving channel that shot through a deep, rocky gorge.

Mayberry turned to watch the retreating beast, but when it had gone only a dozen yards, it turned its head and locked eyes with her. Deftly spinning around, it pawed the earth, lowered its head, and rushed forward. Its knobby horns smashed into the tree trunk with even greater force than before.

Marshall stretched an arm around the tree to grab her wrist and steady her, looping his other one around the trunk for additional purchase. "I hope that didn't hurt him," he said, raising an eyebrow.

The creature backed up a few paces and punched forward again.

Slam.

The tree swayed and quivered.

Relentlessly, the beast continued to charge the tree and drive its sharp horns into the base.

Boom. Boom.

Stirred by the sounds of the turmoil, a few other beasts in the herd left their grazing and trotted over. Emboldened by seeing treed prey, a different beast charged.

Whack.

Another beast bulled into the tree, then another, then another.

Crack. Crack. Crack.

The brittle shriek of splintering wood echoed across the river.

Mayberry screamed as the base of the tree split. She clung tenaciously to the branches as the trunk's top half began falling toward the river. Out of the corner of her eye, she glimpsed one of the smaller beasts trying to halt its charge midstride, but it slipped, then skidded sideways, and its momentum carried it right over the bank.

CHAPTER 16

M ARSHALL'S BRAIN was operating in overdrive. Was it safer to cling to the fractured tree, or should he leap into the water before it splashed in?

The decision was made for him seconds later, as the tangled mass of branches hit the river, sending plumes of water into the air. The rush of cold water was a shock, but when the branches popped back up into the air, he quickly wiped the water from his eyes and looked for Mayberry. He saw that she was still clinging to the branches near him.

Something splashed into the water behind them. When Marshall turned around, he saw a small beast's head appear, then sink under the waves, then pop up again like a cork seconds later. It was using its stumpy legs to dog-paddle toward them.

The swift current swept the tree downriver, and before he

could process it, they were at the edge of the biggest waterfall. The water's roar grew louder as the world tipped away and the branches plummeted down into a vertiginous cloud of white spray and roiling blue water. Their tree became trapped in the whirlpool at the waterfall's base, but after several spins around the bubbling vortex, it tore free and continued rushing downstream, bouncing up and down over the smaller cataracts below.

Miraculously, they had both managed to keep hold of their branches. Bruised, freezing, and terrified, Marshall held on for his life. Mayberry screamed every time they hit a rock, and her hands gripped the branches so tightly that her knuckles had gone white.

Their fun day trip had become a desperate fight for survival. The tree tumbled over the last short drop and rocketed into the narrow channel running through the gorge. The sun's rays were nearly blotted out by the rocky cliffs lining both sides of the river.

"Should w-we let go of the tree and swim-m to shore?" Marshall yelled, shivering violently. Even the most basic decisions were beyond his numb brain's current capacity.

"I d-don't know," Mayberry screamed back. "I d-don't think we can climb out of here."

Marshall leaned his head back and looked up. She was right. The cliff walls were made of sheer rock. They still hadn't lost the beast, either, whose head kept cresting above the waves. It was incredibly persistent and, Marshall suspected, *hungry.* If they left the relative security of the tree, it could catch them in the water, where they were more vulnerable.

"What was th-that?" Mayberry shouted.

For a second, Marshall didn't know what she meant, but then he felt it too—a sharp tug that jerked the tree backward.

"I don't know," he hollered back. "Maybe a branch snagged on something?" He looked back, his eyes straining to pierce through the dark web of branches and shadows.

Suddenly he spotted the problem. It was the cow creature. It had latched onto a branch of the tree with its sharp teeth, and was using its legs and grooved hooves to wrap itself around the tangle of branches to get enough leverage so it could inch closer to Marshall and Mayberry.

"Ummm, Mayberry."

"What?"

Before Marshall could warn her, something started swimming their way, fast, pushing up the water in front of it. The river roiled, and a pewter-gray leviathan burst out. Its massive head had a giant purple eye, as well as a number of smaller ones, and from the sides of its snout sprouted dozens of long, wriggling tentacles. Its jaws opened wide, exposing pointed teeth as big as bowling pins, which clamped onto the beast's hindquarters. Then its rubbery tentacles whipped out to stuff the whole beast down its cavernous throat. The monster glided smoothly beneath the turbid surface . . . then nothing. In a flash, both predator and prey had vanished beneath the murky water.

"What was that?" Mayberry bellowed.

"Some kind of . . . I don't even know."

"I can ad-admit it out loud now, Marshall. We aren't on Earth anymore."

Marshall nodded in agreement and tightened his grip on the tree. The river emerged from the canyon and widened, then began to slow. The cliffs tapered lower, sunshine stroked the river's surface, and finally, the rock walls melted away.

The water turned warmer. Color returned to Mayberry's cheeks, and she stopped shivering.

The river was flanked by muddy banks overgrown with giant rubbery plants, which looked more like jellyfish or coral than Earth flora. Vines tipped with pink flowers as big as dinner plates hung down from trees. Small orange creatures that looked like marsupials, except for their extra sets of arms and legs, skittered up and down the vines, clutching clumps of pale blue nuts. A hairless yellow animal with two chimpanzee-like heads watched them go by from a perch on a high branch, balancing itself with two prehensile tails.

Mayberry finally broke the silence. "The Wishing Tree must be some kind of portal. It sent us to *exactly* the kind of world we asked for."

"Yeah, but the Tree forgot the fun part of our wish," Marshall said. "We're definitely not superheroes. And we can't do magic. But the day is young. Do you think we'll find a way home . . . eventually?"

Mayberry nodded. "If we can get back to the aspen forest,

we'll use the Tree here to take us back to the Tree on Earth. Easy."

Sure, he thought. *Easy.* They were floating in a primordial forest, a hidden Eden, but without the tools or weapons that they needed to help them survive. Marshall was scared, dreading each bend in the river. While nothing had tried to kill them in the last few minutes, he doubted the trend would last long.

The current sped up as they headed into a narrow chute that flowed between two enormous boulders. Waves bounced off the shoulders of the stones, rocking the tree violently.

"*Hang on!*" he screamed at Mayberry.

"*What do you think I'm doing?*"

A thicket of branches near the top of the tree snagged on a sharp outcropping that poked from one of the boulders, bending the whole mass backward. The thicket torqued sharply, then flipped and rolled the tree half over, causing a number of branches to groan and snap. One broken branch spiked down, shearing off the limb Mayberry was clinging to, plunging her into the water.

Marshall pushed off the limb and dove backward. A branch caught at the cuff of his shirt as he stroked toward the surface, but he managed to wrench free. His head burst from the water, and he gratefully sucked in a lungful of air. In the turmoil, his glasses had slipped off and disappeared in the current. Blinking, he strained his watery eyes as he searched anxiously for Mayberry.

The swift current swept the tree downriver . . .

A series of splashes downstream caught his eye. There she was. His wet clothing weighed him down, making every wind-milling stroke difficult, every inch of progress a struggle. But he didn't have enough time to stop and unhitch the backpack; he couldn't afford to lose sight of her. He watched her flailing below him, so bewildered that she was inadvertently trying to swim against the current.

Marshall streaked downstream past her, and then swung around below her. He held out his left arm and let the cur-rent carry her to him. Mayberry had swallowed a lot of water, and her eyes were growing dim. Marshall cupped his right hand under her chin to hold her head above the current, then scissor-kicked for shore as hard as he could until they were floating below a deep-cut bank.

He managed to grab a bunch of the thick grass hanging over the bank's edge, but the force of the current combined with Mayberry's deadweight broke the blades, which sliced into his skin like shards of glass. Blood flowed freely from the wounds, reminding him that there were creatures—some big enough to swallow them whole—lurking in this river.

Exhausted and nearing the end of his endurance, Marshall picked out a muddy, low-lying bank ahead. He gathered his re-maining strength for one final push, knowing this was his last chance, and swam hard for it, holding Mayberry tightly across his chest. He narrowly made it to the bank and reached over to punch his free hand into the mud. He clawed at the slick mud but couldn't gain any purchase, nor could he find anything else that was solid enough to stop his progress downriver. He would never let Mayberry go, which meant they were both doomed.

As Marshall steeled himself for the inevitable end, a pair of huge, hairy hands poked through the underbrush and stretched out to him, palms up. From his vantage point, all he could see were the hands and the long, sinewy muscular arms attached to them. Marshall extended an arm, and soon strong fingers had circled his outreached wrist, closing on it like an iron vise.

Incredibly strong arms and shoulders flexed, easily hauling them both onto the bank before gently releasing them. They were saved. But by what?

As he stared past the riverbank, he saw the huge back of a gray river monster break the surface, then disappear, right at the spot he and Mayberry had just vacated.

CHAPTER 17

"THANKS, MARSHALL," Mayberry said, lying on her back, thirsty for breath. "I w-wasn't ready—didn't have time to catch my breath."

"Yeah," he mumbled, staring over her shoulder. "But we had a little help."

She blinked and looked around. Something rustled the tall bushes nearby. As it emerged, she saw that it was a *who*, not a *what* . . . or maybe it was something in between.

The creature was vaguely humanoid, with a short, sloping forehead, protruding lower jaw, and broad nose. It was the first biped she'd seen here. *Looks like a Bigfoot*, she thought. This one was undoubtedly male, heavily muscled, and at least eight feet tall. His face and body were covered by coarse gray hair marked by bluish stripes. He wore a leathery loincloth held up by a woven rope tied around his waist.

He stared at them, curiosity sparkling in his pale gray eyes, while Mayberry and Marshall took in his polished bone necklace and the leather bindings wrapped around his arms. The creature bent over and lifted up a wooden war hammer that had dozens of sharp ivory spikes jutting from its business end. The spikes looked oddly familiar, and after a moment's reflection, Mayberry realized they might be teeth torn from one of the water carnivores.

Marshall squared his shoulders, straightening up a little taller, and said, "Thank you," adding a courteous bow for emphasis.

The not-quite-human blinked, then made a beckoning gesture with one of his enormous hands. He turned away and began shoving through the brush.

"You want to go with him?" Marshall asked.

"Well, he did save us, and he definitely looks capable of protecting us."

Mayberry noticed that Marshall had lost his glasses. He only needed them for reading, so it wasn't such bad luck; he wouldn't be doing any of that here. He looked cuter without them, but now wasn't the time to think about that, or about the fact that he'd risked his life to save her.

Marshall helped Mayberry up, and they began to follow the strange humanoid picking his way through the thick, thorny bushes. The light breeze whispering through the leaves and the sharp buzzing of strange insects were the only sounds that marked their passage. Finally, they broke into a grassy clearing surrounded by dark green trunks lined with long, sharp spikes. The humanoid stopped. From the shadows, others of his kind, both male and female, emerged into the sunlight. They were all tall and lean and armed with clubs, spears, and other wicked-looking weapons.

The humanoid that had saved them gestured again, then continued walking through the trees. Exhausted and frightened, but feeling lucky to be alive after her harrowing day, Mayberry fell into step behind the creature and Marshall.

CHAPTER 18

THE LEAD CREATURE turned his head and, looking directly at the humans, made a series of trilling noises: his first vocalizations. The voice, especially for a creature his size, was surprisingly high-pitched. His language, if these sounds represented a language, wasn't one that Marshall and Mayberry were able to decipher.

"I don't understand," Mayberry said, shrugging and holding out her hands.

The creature emitted more squeaks. A couple of the others joined in.

"Okay," Marshall said, stepping forward. "This always works in the old Tarzan movies."

He tapped his chest a few times with an index finger.

"Marshall . . . Marshall . . . Marshall." Then he pointed to her. "Mayberry . . . Mayberry."

Mayberry tapped her own chest and repeated her name.

The creatures stopped chattering and listened.

The one who saved them cocked his head slightly, then touched his own chest, answering in a squeaky cough, "Kellain." He repeated it a couple of times, until they could make it out clearly.

"Kellain?" Marshall said, pointing at him.

"Kellain," he echoed.

"Kellain," Mayberry repeated.

The creature bounced excitedly from one foot to the other, and it looked to her like he was smiling.

"Marshall," Kellain said, sounding like he was speaking it with a mouthful of pebbles, but the essence of the name came through.

"Marshall," some of the others echoed.

"Mayberry," Kellain shouted, pointing at her. "Mayberry."

Her name sounded like "Myrthairy" coming from his mouth, but it was close enough. Exchanging names felt like a diplomatic breakthrough. Not quite world peace, but close. Both species' body language got looser, and the threat posed by the creatures' sheer size and numbers—and spiked clubs— started to fade in Mayberry's mind. Still, she guessed that they hadn't yet determined the status of humans in the hierarchy, which sparked another idea.

"Humans," she said, pointing at herself and Marshall, conveying the simple notion she meant to include both of them. "Humans. Humans."

Kellain's face brightened.

He smiled and waved his open hands to encompass his comrades. "Slevicc. Slevicc. Kellain Slevicc. Kendorsh Slevicc. Gallail Slevicc. Lonkee Slevicc."

After more happy head shaking by the Sleviccs, Kellain gestured for Mayberry and Marshall to follow him, then turned into the forest.

They hiked in single file—Kellain, Marshall, Mayberry, and the other Sleviccs—through the cool shade created by the canopy of jellyfish-plants. Mayberry inhaled deeply through her nose, then exhaled slowly through her mouth, a trick to reduce stress she had learned from her mom's yoga teacher. When would this madness finally end? Obviously, playfully goofing around under the Wishing Tree, she'd mistakenly wished herself here, but she'd never ever missed being home with her family this much.

The Sleviccs traveled a well-trod path that twisted through a series of low, grassy hills. They touched Marshall and Mayberry only when coming to aid them on particularly steep sections of the trail, or to help them get past other obstacles for which the small humans needed assistance. Finally, the trail dead-ended at the base of a rough chalk cliff with well-worn petroglyphs of bulky creatures carved into its base, none of which she recognized.

"That'll take some fancy climbing," Marshall remarked, shaking his head as he looked up at the fifteen-foot ascent.

The Slevicc in front stopped at the base of the cliff, looked up at its top, and began to make rapid chopping motions with his hands. Then, he grew taller. It took Mayberry a moment to realize that the Slevicc's head wasn't stretching up from his neck; his feet and body had actually lifted from the ground—he'd floated straight up. In seconds, he'd reached the top of the cliff and stepped onto its ledge.

The next Slevicc male in line made the same slicing motions, then sailed up. A female followed. Kellain gestured for Marshall to go next.

Marshall shook his head and pantomimed a sad face, but Kellain just stood there, waiting patiently.

"Sorry, pal. We don't fly," Mayberry said, shaking her head.

Marshall rolled his shoulders forward and stepped up to the base of the cliff.

"Guess it's worth a try," he said to Mayberry.

He moved his hands, mimicking the Sleviccs' motions as best he could. Nothing happened.

"Now what?" he asked.

Kellain grunted, and two large males came forward. They each grabbed one of Marshall's arms and made the chopping gestures with the hands that weren't holding him.

One instant, the ground was firm and solid beneath Marshall's feet, and then they were floating.

In seconds they were at the top of the ridge, and Marshall stepped forward, planting his sneakers on solid ground again.

Kellain and another Slevicc moved to either side of Mayberry.

"Don't worry," Marshall yelled down, smiling broadly for the first time since being chased by the horned beast.

"Worry?" Her eyes were shining with excitement. "I can't wait." As she wafted upward, held by the Sleviccs, she giggled so hard her cheeks turned pink.

"I really hope we can figure out how to do this on our own," she said to Marshall once her feet hit the earth.

"It would definitely come in handy," he replied smoothly, without a trace of irony.

CHAPTER 19

KELLAIN LED THE WAY to a brush-covered rise a few hundred yards ahead. When he reached the crest of the hill, he froze, then dropped to the ground and flattened his body. He turned with a hand clamped over his mouth and extended his other hand, palm down, and pumped it up and down. All the other Sleviccs dropped, as did Mayberry and Marshall.

Looking over his shoulder with his eyes narrowed, Kellain gently motioned for the two humans to crawl up and join him. They crept forward stealthily, and when Marshall's head was level with Kellain's, he lifted it just enough to peer into the deep valley.

"What do you see?" Mayberry whispered, her head still pressed into the grass.

Marshall pushed forward a bit, so he could make sense of

the jumble of shapes below. Marching along the valley floor was a band of at least fifty brick-red creatures that had squat, heavily muscled bodies. Multicolored markings appeared on their shoulders, backs and arms, but Marshall couldn't tell if they were natural or tattooed.

It took a moment for the kaleidoscope of images to register and unscramble. When they did, his brain recorded the sharp curving tusks that jutted from the creatures' jaws. They were tapered to wicked points, clearly designed to rend and rip. The ferocious-looking army brandished a variety of spears, clubs, hammers, and rough wooden swords. Topping off the horrifying tableau were long stakes topped with bleached skulls being carried by at least a dozen of the creatures. Based on their size and configuration, it seemed like some of the skulls had come from Sleviccs.

As if the appalling scene wasn't scary enough, cougar-size reptiles held by crude collars and leather leashes padded alongside them. The creatures' jagged brown fangs were pressed low to the ground as they sniffed the earth like bloodhounds.

This was clearly a war party on the march. Marshall was so taken aback that he couldn't utter a word, so Mayberry inched forward and lifted her head to assess the scene herself.

After the troop of beasts disappeared, Kellain grimaced and shook his head. "Heeturs," he grumbled unhappily.

After this incident, their procession crept away from the rise, then got up silently; there was no more of the Sleviccs' comforting chatter.

Hours later, as they emerged from a thicket of blue-stalked plants, Marshall spotted a village at the top of a narrow plateau. They walked toward a thick perimeter of interwoven thorn bushes, which protected the village from intruders. The only visible entrance was a tall wooden door bristling with spikes; it swung open at Kellain's shrill call.

Marshall had anticipated primitive dwellings—lean-tos, or maybe crude mud huts. Instead he saw ample, well-constructed homes that resembled Mongol yurts. Their outer walls were expertly thatched, many with lengths of colored fabric woven into them, and the roofs were made from curved wood shingles fastened together by braided ropes. As they passed an open door, he saw that the dwelling's interior walls were painted with elegant, colorful organic patterns. Bright banners fluttered on poles between the buildings, creating a carnival atmosphere.

More Sleviccs emerged from the buildings, shouting, smiling, and warmly embracing the returnees.

Mayberry clutched Marshall's hand tighter.

"Look," she said, subtly tilting her head.

He followed her gaze to a Slevicc wearing a rusty canteen slung on a ragged, military-style belt—definitely manufactured. It reminded him of photos he'd seen of World War I soldiers' canteens.

"There's more." Mayberry pointed to a lodge whose exterior wall incorporated a section of buffalo skins decorated with beadwork. Another displayed a round Native American shield, a beaded breastplate, and other Plains Indian–style antiques.

"They've met humans before," he said softly.

"Right," Mayberry said. "But is that good or bad?"

"I don't know."

Mayberry pointed at the colorful banners. "It looks like there's a festival going on or something. Maybe they need a king and queen like they have during Mardi Gras. Or maybe they want to worship us as gods." She smiled. "Or as a goddess and her faithful sidekick."

"Could be," Marshall said. "I'm ready to sit on the stairs near your throne, as long as you feed me while I'm sidekicking."

"I'm hungry, too," Mayberry said, scanning the village for signs of something edible.

CHAPTER 20

FIVE SLEVICCS headed their way. Kellain stepped in front of the party and cheeped while gesturing wildly with his hands, but after some fast-paced conversation, he stopped talking and lowered his head as if they had convinced him they were right. He stood aside, and the rest of them turned and walked toward the humans.

"So I guess it's not time to crown us after all," Marshall said, squaring his shoulders and mentally preparing for whatever was next.

The two lead Sleviccs bent over and gently grabbed Marshall under his armpits. When he started to twist away, their grip turned to iron.

"Hey, let go," he screamed.

When two more clasped Mayberry's shoulders, she began

kicking, swearing, and trying to wrest herself free. Resistance was futile, though, so she finally went limp, forcing them to carry her.

As the Sleviccs hauled them across the camp, Mayberry spotted a large round cage made from fiber ropes and wooden slats. As they got closer, she noted two pinkish piglike creatures huddled in the corner. The animals stared at the approaching group with fearful light green eyes set over protruding snouts, but the similarity to Earth pigs ended there. The creatures stood upright on thin legs that ended in small hooves and wore rough loincloths around their waists. Their front . . . arms, yes, arms, she decided . . . ended in clawed three-fingered paws. One of them had a metal ring piercing its nose, and the other wore three metal ear studs. The animals squealed in terror as they passed the cage. One covered its face with its paws, while the other scooted backward until its body pressed hard into the wooden bars. They were clearly terrified of the Sleviccs.

Marshall and Mayberry were brought to a nicely appointed thatch hut that had numerous eye-level ventilation holes cut into the walls. One Slevicc pulled the door open, while the others ushered them in and closed the door behind them. Marshall stumbled and fell onto his knees in the soft dirt. His outstretched legs tripped Mayberry, too, and she slammed into his back so hard they both landed in a jumbled pile. She sat up, covered with dirt, and scraped a hunk of hair out of her face.

The ground slipped away beneath Marshall's feet.

"This is *not* how you treat a goddess," she said, idly tracing her name in the dust with a finger. "This is my fault. I was the one who pressured you to come into the Mystery Forest with me, even though I knew it might be dangerous. I just . . . didn't really believe it."

Marshall sat next to her and smoothed her name out of the dust. "You didn't *make* me go with you, and Nostradamus himself couldn't have predicted that we'd end up in this ungodly mess."

Mayberry smiled at him gratefully, blew out a puff of air, and relaxed her shoulders. Then she laid her head on Marshall's lap, while he leaned his back against the wall of the hut and closed his eyes. In seconds, the two of them were dozing.

Her eyelids fluttered open when she smelled smoke wafting in, carrying with it the sweet scent of roasting ham. Mayberry wasn't ordinarily a meat eater, but she was starving, and a hefty slab of grilled pork ribs sounded better than beet salad or a soy burger. Her mouth began to water. She peered out of one of the ventilation holes, looking for the source of the appetizing smell.

The sun had almost set, and the sky was turning deep blue, edging into purple. On the far side of the grassy circle that marked the center of the village, she spotted a small stone-ringed campfire whose bright red flames were licking a long hunk of spitted meat.

Her jaw dropped.

She turned back to Marshall and shook him awake. Clutching his arm, she dragged him over to one of the ventilation holes and pointed.

His eyes followed the line of her index finger to the spit. "I am *sooo* hungry," he said through parched lips. "I could eat that whole porker."

"That is *not* a pig roasting. Look at the earrings. It's one of those beasties from the cage. No wonder they were so scared."

"Oh my God," Marshall said, sitting down heavily. "That is so messed up."

Mayberry sat, too, and soon her tears were making dark spots on her dusty jeans. "Th-they—" Her voice folded and cracked. She swallowed, trying again. "The Sleviccs are going to eat us. Those relics we saw are probably hunting trophies."

Before now she hadn't thought it was possible for her day to get any worse, but now they were trapped at the wrong end of this planet's food chain. It seemed that they were destined to become human barbecue.

CHAPTER 21

MARSHALL WAS NEAR his own breaking point, too. He reached out and drew Mayberry into his arms, cradling her like a newborn. She burrowed her head into his chest and started to bawl. He couldn't explain why, and it didn't make sense, but his spirits lifted. As long as he had breath left, he wasn't going to give up, fall apart, or stop fighting to save her. Failure wasn't an option.

"Look," he said softly. "We don't actually know what the Sleviccs have planned for us. They've treated us like friends, not food. Let's find Kellain and try to figure out what's going on."

When he tried to push the door open, he discovered that it had been locked from the outside. This wasn't good news.

"Uh, Mayberry, we're locked in," Marshall said, waving a hand at the door.

Mayberry rolled her eyes, all cried out. "Doesn't surprise me. They obviously don't like their food free range."

From the ventilation holes, they could see that the Sleviccs had removed their roasted meat from the spits and were laboring in well-coordinated units to toss logs onto a bonfire, which threw plumes of flame up into the dark sky. The thick gray tendrils of smoke spitting from the bonfire created a smoggy haze that quickly blanketed the whole village. Observing the Sleviccs' frenzied action, Marshall realized far more Sleviccs than he had first imagined lived here. As the moon crept over the stockade, Marshall was able to count more than a hundred individuals coming and going.

Mayberry gasped as she peered through her ventilation hole.

"What is it?" Marshall asked, stepping quickly to her side.

"If that's the moon rising . . . then what is that?" Her finger shifted, identifying a second orb that sat next to the first one, at approximately the same height above the horizon.

"That's . . . the other moon," Marshall said, shaking his head.

"And what about that one?"

A small asteroid, hard to discern in the fading light, sat captured between the gravity fields of the moons. Marshall and Mayberry looked at each other and nodded. Anything was possible now.

The Sleviccs gathered around the bonfire, arranging themselves on the ground a few feet apart in neat concentric circles.

With legs crossed and eyes closed, they swayed together and began a deep rhythmic humming. Together, as one, they levitated, their bodies bobbing gently at various heights in the air. It looked to Marshall from their posture like they were meditating.

Suddenly it occurred to Marshall that they didn't *have* to stay in the hut. They might be the Sleviccs' postmeditation entrée, or they might not, but it was stupid to wait around to find out. He dug into his beat-up backpack, pulled out his Swiss Army knife, and held it up for Mayberry to see. He pointed at the thatch wall and made a scissor motion with his fingers. Mayberry jumped to her feet and went to a ventilation hole to keep an eye on the Sleviccs. Marshall stepped over to the wall farthest from the bonfire, unfolded the knife's serrated blade, and went to work.

"How's it going, Marshall?" Mayberry asked a few minutes later.

"It's going. The fiber is tougher than it looks—it's like cutting through tin."

He continued to cut until he had an opening about three feet high and two feet wide, just big enough for them to squeeze through. From there it was just a few dozen steps to the gate, where freedom beckoned.

"Okay," he grunted. "Time to get the hell out of here."

CHAPTER 22

MARSHALL HELPED Mayberry squeeze out of the hole, then led the way, trying to run while crouching low at the same time.

They unlatched and crept through the gate, the three moons lighting the landscape well enough for them to distinguish the shapes ahead. Below the plateau, the sounds of a primal jungle night echoed: croaking, hoots, whistles, and deep grunts.

The duo briskly backtracked along the trail they'd come in on. When they reached the small chalk cliff, they carefully circled and climbed down the gently sloping hill that faced its right side. After an hour or so, they emerged onto the flat section where the trail intersected the dank forest.

Marshall waved her to a halt. Mayberry bent over with her hands on her knees and looked up at him quizzically.

"I want us to be able to see where we're walking before we go in that forest." He pawed around his backpack, finally pulling out a small LED flashlight.

"Ooh, a flashlight," Mayberry said admiringly. "That's nearly as good as food. But I'd trade it for half a PB-and-J sandwich."

"Too bad we ate our snacks this morning," Marshall said as he clicked the power button a couple of times. Nothing. He slapped the flashlight against his palm. That usually did the trick. Not this time.

"It's not working."

"Maybe Earth technology doesn't work here, period."

"I thought it was worth trying . . ." It was getting harder for him to stay positive. It was darker outside now, and their plight seemed hopeless.

"Anything else you need from there?" Mayberry asked, looking over Marshall's shoulder into the backpack. "We've got to get going. Once we find the river, we can follow it upstream to the forest."

He tossed the dead flashlight inside his backpack and rummaged around to remind himself what other supplies he'd brought. "Okay. I have weatherproof matches, duct tape, a flint, a signal mirror, an emergency foil blanket, fishhooks, and string. And I have the repository of all necessary outdoor knowledge: *The Boy Scout Handbook*."

He suddenly had an idea. "Let's get back to caveman basics," he exclaimed, pointing at a bunch of fallen tree limbs. "We'll make torches.

"There's plenty of wood. Find some dry, broom-size sticks," he instructed.

Mayberry searched the forest floor and found two fairly straight pieces of wood that were slightly thicker than a broomstick and about four feet long. Marshall bunched dried branches onto one end of the wood and duct-taped them on. Then he shredded some of the *Handbook's* pages for tinder and wove them into the branches sprouting out. He held a match to the paper, which glowed bright red and lit up the branches. Beaming, he fired up Mayberry's torch too.

With the torchlight to guide them, the sort of familiar trail underneath their feet, and the Sleviccs far behind, their mood lifted. An hour ago they'd been prisoners and maybe entrées. Now they were free and headed back toward the Tree that could take them home.

After an hour of fast-paced walking, Mayberry slowed and held up a hand for Marshall to stop. Breathing hard, she bent over and squeezed her aching calves. Marshall was happy to take a break, too; his lungs were on fire and his legs were shaky. Mayberry turned in small circles, one hand on her waist, catching her breath. In the torchlight Marshall saw her face was red and splotchy from exertion.

"You okay?"

"Fine, just . . . a bit . . . winded . . . is all."

He was about to tell her that he felt the same when he heard Something Very Big crashing through the forest behind them.

"Run," he hollered. "Now!"

CHAPTER 23

MAYBERRY RACED down the trail, her aches and pains forgotten. It sounded like a Hummer was bulldozing through brick walls behind them. She sprinted down the trail for what seemed like at least half a mile, with low branches whipping her face and body mercilessly the whole time. Finally, the noise quieted, and she and Marshall went from running, to jogging, then stopped. Her legs were jelly, and her chest ached. Dizzy, she stumbled into Marshall, grabbing his shoulder for support.

"Is it gone?" she mumbled, gasping hard for air.

"I don't hear it," Marshall said, leaning on his torch. "But I can't hear much of anything except my head exploding."

"That's good," she grunted, her lips quirking into a thin smile. "I'm tired of running." As her heartbeat slowed, she heard the splashing and tumbling of water. "You hear that, Marshall? We must have found the river. Let's go."

Just a few steps in, she caught sight of a shaggy brown head thrusting out of the bushes, watching her. A long red tongue flicked rapidly in and out of its slavering jaws, which were lined by pointed teeth. She screamed and stepped backward.

Apparently this was the same creature they'd heard bashing through the woods behind them. It had circled around to cut them off, which meant it was capable of stealth and strategy. The prodigious monster's body was as bulky as two elephants, and had a number of powerfully muscled legs sprouting from a long, hairy torso. Its maw stretched open wide enough to swallow Mayberry whole. Six red eyes—two the size of coffee mugs—stared malevolently at her as it flowed forward, smooth as a centipede, to block her passage.

As Marshall stepped up beside her, Mayberry knew she was about to die. A glowing red light crackled out of her right palm, and the torch burned brighter, then shot out of her hand and sank into the matted fur behind the creature's neck.

Whoosh.

As if its body had been soaked in kerosene, the monster exploded in a blazing inferno. Howling in pain, it threw itself down and rolled through the brush, crushing everything in its path as it tried to extinguish the red-hot flames that engulfed it.

Marshall grabbed Mayberry's hand and pulled her away from the blaze.

"*Run,*" he yelled for the second time in minutes.

The creature's nightmarish screams, the roaring flames, and the black soot rising into the air spurred Mayberry's exhausted body forward. When they finally broke past the edge of the smoke, she saw the fire washing the sky behind them, painting a false red-and-yellow sunrise.

Marshall shouted encouragement over his shoulder. "Keep going," he said. "Forest fires can travel much faster than you think."

Before he could whip his head back around, he missed a sharp bend in the trail, tripped, and barreled headfirst into the darkness. His torch sailed in a bright arc, smacking into the earth right behind the spot where he had disappeared. Mayberry scooped it up without missing a step and followed the path his body had leveled through the bushes.

Suddenly screeching to a halt, she threw her arms wildly out sideways to catch her balance. She was teetering precariously on the edge of the riverbank.

Marshall hadn't been as lucky. He was sliding down the steep, slippery bank, his fingers plowing furrows in the soft brown mud. With his arms and legs spread-eagled, he managed to punch his hands deep enough into the goop to pin his body to the bank, but his red sneakers were dangling dangerously over the edge and splashing in the water. As soon as the powerful current sucked him off his tenuous perch, she would never see him again.

Mayberry drove the torch's pointed base into the top of the soft mud as deep as she could, then quickly grasped it and shimmied down the bank until one of her shoes bumped into Marshall's shoulder.

"Grab it," she screamed.

He fired his right hand out of the mud and snagged one of her ankles, which he used to haul himself up and over her body until he reached her shoulders. His body's weight pushed hers deeper into the mud. He arched a sneaker onto her left shoulder and, using it for leverage, thrust his other leg up and over the top of the bank, where he squirmed to freedom.

He instantly flipped around onto his stomach and wiggled the toes of his sneakers as deep as he could into the top of the bank. He stretched his arms down, grabbed Mayberry's wrists, and heaved her back up.

Breathing so hard they were quivering, they held each other tight.

"Thank you. I thought I was dead," Marshall said, squeezing her even tighter. "And you actually *blew up* that monster. How did you *do* that?"

Mayberry shook her head. "I have no idea. Did you see how my hand went red before the torch shot out of it?"

"That was incredible. Your hand *glowed*," Marshall replied. "I guess one of us got the magic we wished for," he said.

"Maybe. It all happened so fast, it's hard to know for sure," she said.

She dropped her mud-covered head onto his chest and looked up into his amber-flecked eyes. She felt a sudden impulse to kiss him, but the smelly mud coating his face and hers held her back, so she settled for a hug instead.

He stroked her muddy head with his muddy hand. "Well, at least we found the river."

CHAPTER 24

THEY RESTED FOR A WHILE, bathed in the light cast by the torch. Finally, Marshall got up and jerked the torch out of the mud, then reached down and pulled Mayberry up. The two went trudging along the riverbank while a pale band of yellow light started to peek over the horizon.

"The sun's coming up," Marshall said. He could see clusters of springy mushrooms stair-stepping up the massive trees near the river. Since they didn't have machetes to hack through the jungle, the only way they could travel safely was along the riverbank.

"Or *a* sun," Mayberry corrected. "I only saw one yesterday, but who knows?"

Marshall didn't care how many suns rose as long as they found something to eat soon. His stomach was about to start consuming his body from the inside out. Assuming, of course, that he didn't drop dead from exhaustion first.

As the sun poked over the trees, he scanned the horizon. During their rough ride down the river the day before, they'd dropped down a number of waterfalls, then spurted into a canyon. He had no idea how far they had already traveled back upriver, but they hadn't reached any waterfalls yet, so they still had a long hike ahead of them. At a small, placid bay, they took a short break to drink, fill Marshall's canteen, and do their best to clean up. When they set off again, they walked slowly to conserve their scant energy.

"Is that a clearing?" Mayberry asked peering ahead. "Maybe the beginning of a meadow?"

Shafts of light sliced into what appeared to be open ground ahead. Suddenly, a band of familiar-looking silhouettes stepped into the sunlight, which danced on their shoulders and glinted off the long spikes embedded in their war clubs.

"Oh, *no*," he gulped. "Sleviccs."

There were five of them, and they were ready for battle. He recognized a few from the village by their markings and dress.

"Yeah, they're Sleviccs, all right," Mayberry said, crestfallen. "And they look pissed off. Let's *go*."

Mayberry spun around, taking off at a feeble sprint back the way they had come. Marshall followed a fraction of a second later. The Sleviccs burst into action, shouting gutterally and pursuing them with huge loping strides. They heard the thunder of heavy feet gaining on them, punctuated by the creak of leather and the jangle of clanking bone.

CHAPTER 25

MARSHALL'S LONG-LEGGED STRIDES zipped him past Mayberry, but when he heard her cry, he whirled around just as a meaty Slevicc hand slammed into the small of his back. Marshall stumbled sideways and smacked into the trunk of a jellyfish plant. His body broke through the plant's thin membrane, and a stinging fluid splashed into his eyes. He thrashed out of the plant trying desperately to blink his eyes back to normal, but he could barely make out the Sleviccs. As his eyes cleared, he saw that Mayberry was crouching on the ground, with Sleviccs positioned on both sides. Although they looked dangerous, they held their weapons limply by their sides, clearly not poised to strike.

Marshall groped along the ground for a weapon of his own until his hand closed on a stout branch. As he regained his feet, a white glow started to form around his fingers, and

Its maw stretched open wide enough to swallow Mayberry whole.

he felt an enormous pulse of power ignite a rush of adrenaline. Before he consciously absorbed what was happening and fought back, a deep voice sounded, resonating loudly enough to muffle all competing noises around it.

The Sleviccs backed up when they heard the sound, and closed ranks into a tight combat formation.

Marshall, gripping the branch, made sure Mayberry was still behind him and spun to face the newcomer.

His brain recoiled. This green-skinned . . . male . . . whatever . . . looked like a giant, muscular centaur that stood upright like a troll. Two long, prehensile tails sprouted from his hindquarters. One tail flicked forward like a whip to shoo a bug from his cheek.

The thing's oval head was essentially human in structure—at least he had two eyes, a nose, and a mouth—but dark cavities occupied the space usually reserved for ears, and his big eyes were a vibrant purple, topped by thick white eyebrows. Wispy white hair tinged with gray stood out in tufts on top of his head, and a long beard covered his broad chin. Marshall sensed a cold, frightening savagery in the planes of his face. The monster's mouth was open wide enough to engulf a whole chicken in one bite.

His prodigiously muscled weightlifter's torso supported a protruding belly, and his shoulders were wider than a door. He had two sets of ham-hock arms, each ending in four-fingered hands with dirty brown claws. Attired in stained leather panels, with metal scimitars dangling at his hips and two daggers hanging from scabbards in front of his belly, the creature appeared ready for action.

Whoa.

He wasn't traveling alone. There was a human standing a couple of yards behind him. The man was slightly taller than Marshall, but much older, with rumpled red hair, a sharp nose, and a bluish birthmark on his right cheek. Dressed in neat, hand-stitched leather garments, he clutched a braided leash attached to the collar of a furry turtle-shaped creature that was as wide as a hippo, with a long spiked tail. Hemp ropes secured a jumbled pile of bundles strapped onto its broad back.

Marshall's first thought was that this mismatched pair was going to try to rescue them, but the human didn't look very happy to see Marshall and Mayberry.

For a millisecond, a flash of recognition flitted through Marshall's mind, and he wanted to ask *Do I know you?* but the question was so ludicrous he dismissed it and substituted, "What's going on?"

The man didn't respond. He wouldn't even make eye contact with Marshall, but was using frantic hand signals to warn the Sleviccs to back off.

Troll-man and the Sleviccs grunted furiously at each other, then the Sleviccs began to screech and shake their weapons defiantly.

Troll-man thrust out his upper arms, and a brilliant brown luminescence erupted from the four thick fingers on his hands. Waves of brown power struck the ground in front of the Sleviccs, causing dirt, rocks, and nearby trees to erupt as though they were caught in an earthquake. The Sleviccs scattered, trying to protect their heads, but more than one suffered brutal wounds from the flying debris.

Troll-man twirled his lower fingers, and a white essence hissed out and raced to a dead tree trunk on the ground nearby. The fifteen-foot-long trunk rose and began whirling like a helicopter blade, then catapulted toward the remaining Sleviccs. One tried to levitate over it, but the lethal trunk walloped him like a giant baseball bat. In seconds, the landscape was littered with dead or dying Sleviccs.

Mayberry clutched Marshall, goggle-eyed, and the sheer brutality of what they were seeing made Marshall retch. He bent over, the acid rising from the cauldron of his stomach burning his throat. When he lifted his head, he saw a Slevvic who didn't retreat or run for his life, as common sense dictated, but charged forward and threw his spear at Troll-man, who deflected it with a pulse of orange miasma. Finally, the whirling trunk's deadly assault caught the remaining Slevicc and smacked into his shins, knocking him off his feet.

CHAPTER 26

MAYBERRY HAD NEVER SEEN a dead body before. And now there were four. The only word that came to mind as she watched the horrific encounter was *slaughter*. Troll-man butchered the Sleviccs with an enthusiastic abandon bordering on glee.

Now only one Slevicc remained, an old graying male. He faced the Troll-man and got on his knees, tears streaming down his cheeks as he wept for his fallen comrades.

Mayberry's eyes filled with water, too. She turned to Troll-man's human companion. "Tell him the Slevicc surrenders!"

The man's blank blue eyes met hers briefly, then shifted away. Glowering, Troll-man flicked his lower fingers. A viscous gray liquid sped from them and flowed over the ground like quicksilver.

The old Slevicc closed his eyes and hummed, preparing for death. The gray liquid seeped into the ground around a massive boulder, soaked into the earth, and disappeared. Then it reappeared under the boulder, pushing it out of the ground. Troll-man twirled his fingers again, and the liquid shot the boulder up into the air, moving it until it was positioned directly above the Slevicc's bowed head. With a twitch of Troll-man's finger, the liquid vanished, and the boulder plummeted to earth. The murderous blow smashed the helpless Slevicc, leaving only his splayed feet protruding from the rock.

Mayberry screamed in dismay.

Marshall grabbed her and pushed her face into his neck, trying to comfort her and muffle her cries at the same time. Inviting the Troll-man's attention seemed like a bad idea.

"It's over now," he said quietly.

Mayberry looked up at Marshall with a tearstained face. "He just . . . *butchered* those Sleviccs."

"I know," he said, wiping sweat from his forehead with the back of his hand. "And we have no idea what he's got planned for us. We should try to communicate with him. I'm not sure if the human speaks English, and it's hard to say if he'd help us even if he does."

Marshall took a deep breath. He stepped carefully over the rapidly decomposing bodies of the Sleviccs and picked his way toward the Troll-man with his hands up and palms out.

"Hello," he said, his voice wavering.

Troll-man's ferocious reptilian eyes squinted into narrow slits. One of his upper hands tugged his beard while his two lower hands fingered the daggers slung in front of his belly.

"Yu magik," Troll-man declared in a deep guttural voice, gesturing at Marshall.

"Magic?" he dumbly echoed. *He speaks our language.* His brain scrambled to process this revelation.

"Yu magik. Yu magik?" Troll-man shouted louder and louder, looking angry.

What? He wasn't sure what surprised him more: that this creature spoke broken English, or that he thought that Marshall was capable of magic.

"You mean . . . can we do magic?" Marshall squeaked as he struggled to find his voice. "Maybe, but . . ."

Troll-man cocked one white eyebrow as his lips turned down in a disgusted scowl.

"Sleviccs no kep umans fom Monga, yu no kep magik fom Monga," he grunted, using one of his filthy hands to wipe the slobber dripping from his mouth. Then he dropped his four hands to his sides so fast they were impossible to follow. One instant they were empty; the next, two hands held the hilts of swords, two more gripped daggers, and his massive bulk was rushing toward Marshall.

CHAPTER 27

EVEN THOUGH his brain ordered him to grab Mayberry and run, Marshall's feet grew roots. He heard the fearsome blades slashing through the air, the loud drumming of hooves, and the sound of surf crashing on the beach—the surf noise being created by the rush of blood to his brain, which would soon be splashed across the landscape.

The foul smell of Troll-man's body unglued Marshall's legs, but he backed up clumsily and tripped over a rock. As he fell, he desperately thrust his hands out and screamed, "Get back."

In a flash, the air around his fingers changed color, and a jolt of bright white light burst from them and crashed into Troll-man with the force of a truck. The blow belted him backward and into the air, his limbs flailing wildly as the blades flew out of his hands.

Mayberry ran toward Marshall while Troll-man was still caught in the white light. One of the daggers whizzed by her head, perilously close to her left ear.

In midair Troll-man curled into a tight ball, wrapping his limbs and tails around his torso, then crashed into the earth with a thud. His body rolled backward, carving a dark furrow into the ground.

This exchange made all the other impossible wonders Marshall and Mayberry had experienced seem as mundane as a chess club meeting at Eden Grove High.

Troll-man released his limbs and tails, uncurled, and rocked back onto his feet. He was dirty but unscathed, and his stolid face remained blank and unreadable.

Mayberry tugged Marshall to his feet as Troll-man began to swagger back toward them. He gathered up all his swords and daggers as he came, but instead of facing Marshall again, his purple gaze locked on Mayberry.

"Yu magik?" he said, flicking one of his tails near her right side, the other by her left.

Mayberry set her jaw and crossed her arms over her chest. "No magic for you."

"Yu magik?" he snarled again.

Mayberry grasped Marshall's hand tightly and said nothing.

Troll-man raised his swords, swishing them through the air for effect before leaping forward.

Neither of them knew if their magic would work again, but

they pushed out their arms together and screamed "Get back," as Troll-man rolled forward. Bolts of bright power ribboned from Marshall's hands and red miasma from Mayberry's. The colors merged into a thick stream of pink repelling power that pummeled Troll-man, tossing him up and back twice as far as Marshall's magic had before.

Unharmed, the creature rose, methodically gathering his weapons and slipping them back into their scabbards. His face twisted into a wry half grin, and the furrows in his forehead vanished.

Troll-man approached Marshall and Mayberry calmly, his weapons sheathed. "Goot," he said, pointing at each of them with a separate pair of hands. "Goot, yu. Yu myne. Yu myne keedluns."

"What?" Marshall whispered to Mayberry.

"I think he's trying to say that we're his kids."

Marshall shuddered. "Yeah, that's what it sounds like to me, too. I guess that's a good thing," he said. "After all, he did save us from the Sleviccs. Before he killed them all."

"Yeah, there is that. He could have killed us, too, but it seems like he was just testing us for magic, which we do have. Maybe it's an ability that only comes to us when we think we're in mortal danger."

Marshall nodded. That seemed about right.

"Seet, seet," Troll-man said, pointing to the ground.

Marshall suddenly remembered the human who had been watching them. He looked over at him and raised his hands, as if to ask what was going on. The man twitched his shoulders and subtly shook his head.

"Okay," Marshall said. That *no* didn't really help them right now, but at least they might be able to communicate later.

He and Mayberry sat on the ground in front of the creature, with the grim remains of the dead Sleviccs behind them.

"Me Monga," Troll-man informed them, rapidly pounding his chest with his upper arms. "Me Monga, keedluns no ferget Monga."

Marshall elbowed Mayberry and whispered, "Unlikely."

Monga opened his enormous mouth, flashing a set of stained square teeth that looked sharp enough to peel the hide off an alligator.

"Unn li-ikely," he said, imitating Marshall. It was frightening that he could hear them whisper, but fortunate that he didn't understand Marshall's impudence.

"Yu seet, Monga show . . ."

CHAPTER 28

SINCE THEY HAD PASSED his reckless field test, Monga was treating them like friends. Although, technically, they were his prisoners, it seemed the tide of bizarre events might have finally turned in their favor. Maybe this terrible beast would help them get home. Mayberry hated this world. One creature had tried to stomp her to death, another had attempted to gulp her down its huge maw, and others, who walked on two feet no less, had planned to roast her over a spit. She couldn't get back to Earth soon enough. Having Marshall with her was the only thing keeping her sane. Right now, she was comforted by the fact that he sat next to her, gently holding her hand as Monga began to perform.

He mumbled garbled gibberish under his breath. His legs moved back and forth with surprising grace while his hooves kicked up small clouds of dust. Mayberry kept expecting his ungainly bulk to pitch over, but Monga kept all his movements comfortably balanced, gesticulating rapidly with his hands to form carefully choreographed motions as his hooves pranced merrily along.

The bright yellow sun was climbing higher into the sky, and its warmth washed over Mayberry, making her sleepy eyes droop. It took her a second to realize that wherever Monga moved his fingers, a glowing, leaf-green thread appeared. He began to craft double, then triple, overlapping strands of translucent green energy, which hung delicately in the air like a magical spiderweb. Reaching into a leather pouch on his belt marked with intricate red curlicues, Monga withdrew a bright red powder. Pinching it carefully between two thick fingers, he sprinkled the red grains across the strands. With a quick dart of another finger, the red dust glowed faintly, then seeped into the green web. Two red coils formed inside the maze, then began to spin counterclockwise.

Shocked, Mayberry began to laugh—a bit hysterically— with delight. After all, they *had* wished for a world with magic, and Monga was putting on a class-A performance.

He grunted a brief chant while flicking the fingers of his upper right and left hands, and the red coils transformed into bolts of whirling neon-red light. The bolts uncoiled like snakes, darted out of the green vortex, and sped toward the humans, who ducked and held their hands over their faces.

Monga's distorted mouth creaked into a smile as the darts

swooped around and splattered onto Marshall's and Mayberry's backs.

Mayberry's head bucked forward as the center of her upper back began to burn. Marshall cried out and began pawing wildly at the same spot between his shoulder blades.

"What did you do?" Marshall said to Monga, who declined to answer. He was humming contentedly while using his dirty claws to pick his teeth.

Mayberry had seen the pain on Marshall's face and gestured for him to turn so she could examine his back. His clothes were unmarked.

"Nothing," Mayberry whispered. "There's nothing there."

Marshall bent forward, tugging up his jacket and shirt. "But something *burned* us."

"Let me check," she said, lifting his shirt farther up. She gasped when she saw the angry red swirl engraved on the skin. "It looks like a fresh scar in the shape of a swirl. Does it still hurt?"

"No. It burned like crazy, but just for a few seconds."

She pulled up her sweater and T-shirt, twisting around to reveal her back to him. "Take a look?"

Marshall sighed. "Same thing. A red spiral, right between your shoulder blades."

She waved her hands to get Monga's attention. "What did you do to us?"

"Yu Monga's." He jerked an upper thumb toward the redheaded human. "Saim Urrn."

"Same as . . . your name is Urrn?" Marshall asked, turning to the man. "You speak English, Urrn?"

Without acknowledging Marshall, Urrn continued gazing into the dust by his feet. For the time being, Mayberry was less interested in Urrn than in whatever Monga had just done to them.

"What do you mean, we *belong* to you?"

"Monga mark. No tak off. Keedluns go, Monga find."

Squaring her shoulders, Mayberry stood up with her hands clenched and stepped toward Monga. She was faint, starving, and exhausted. Her weary eyes were sore, her head ached, her brain was barely functioning, and she was fed up.

"Take the marks *off*," she said. "I mean it. You do what I say or . . ."

While she was threatening him, Monga scribbled a complex yellow pattern in the air with the index fingers of his upper hands. He flicked the fingers, causing an innocuous-looking trail of yellow sparks to race toward Mayberry. The sparks curved around her body before splashing into her mark. Pain surged through the nerves between her shoulder blades, then tore through the rest of her body like lightning. Involuntarily arching her spine, she fell into the grass and began to writhe, trying desperately to escape the agony.

Marshall wheeled to attack Monga with the only spell he knew. But before he could fire it, Monga blew air over his fingertips, conjuring a gray wind spell so powerful that it undercut Marshall's legs, tumbling him roughly to the ground. Then

Monga cast the same yellow spell again and lit up Marshall's mark. Marshall howled and threw himself on the ground next to Mayberry, rolling back and forth in an attempt to extinguish the intense pain emanating from the neon-red mark now glowing through his shirt.

Excruciating as it had been when it first hit, the pain kept growing and spreading through Mayberry's body like poison. It felt as though thousands of fire ants were devouring her flesh from the inside.

Monga made a sharp, chopping gesture with his index fingers, and the pain stopped. He'd just given them their first and most important magic lesson: this was what would happen if they tried to defy him.

Covered in sweat, Mayberry struggled to sit up, terrified that Monga might suddenly decide that releasing more pain would reinforce his point.

Water streamed from the corner of Marshall's bloodshot eyes as he struggled to his feet, his legs trembling.

Monga gazed smugly at Marshall and Mayberry, his purple eyes full of anticipation, waiting to see if there was anything else they wanted to share with him.

Urrn continued to look away.

"We're his slaves now," Mayberry whispered. "He just made that perfectly clear," she said, pressing the heels of her hands against her eyes.

"You think he can really use magic to track us, and do this to us no matter where we are?"

"I wouldn't bet against it."

Marshall tilted his head toward Urrn. "Now we know that he's a slave, too. Who knows how long Monga's had him."

"Absolutely," she replied, feeling more helpless than she ever had before. Scratches, shallow cuts, and bruises covered her body, she smelled disgusting, and so did her filthy clothes. She had barely enough energy to move. Every time she began to sense a tiny bit of hope, things only got worse.

It resembled an impossibly big, incredibly muscular four-armed centaur.

CHAPTER 29

GNORING HIS NEW SLAVES, Monga signaled to Urrn that it was time to leave the clearing.

"Uuth," Urrn said to his pet, tugging sharply on its leather leash. The creature ambled happily after him, this planet's version of a faithful sheepdog.

Marshall was glad to leave the dead Sleviccs behind. Their bodies had become puddles of putrid yellow gore pooled around piles of bones. Marshall and Mayberry picked their way around the remains, but Monga had no such compunction, freely crunching and cracking Slevicc bones with his hooves as he moved toward the river trail.

"Soon dair," he grunted.

"I hope there's food where we stop," Mayberry mumbled at Marshall. "I keep thinking I'm going to black out."

"Just hang on," Marshall said as he stumbled wearily along the path. "He wants to use us—he's not going to starve us to death."

After a short, steep climb, they reached a grassy knoll that overlooked the river flowing twenty feet below them. Marshall heard the familiar thunder of the rapids echoing up the steep stone cliffs.

Once they'd stopped, Urrn untied the packages that the creature carried on its back. Marshall was amazed at the sheer volume of *stuff* the beast was able to haul. Urrn pulled tent poles and a waxed woven cloth off the mound that was now piled on the ground. They helped Urrn put up Monga's outsized cloth tent. He used crude hand signals to direct Mayberry and Marshall during the setup. The tent's faded brown weave was covered with multicolored patterns that mirrored the curlicues on his belt pouches. Occasionally, as they pitched the rest of the camp, Urrn drew his own patterns in the air and flicked his fingers, using magic to speed up the process.

While all this frenetic activity was going on, Monga leaned his right haunch casually against a large boulder. After watching them scramble for a while, he withdrew a packet of crushed leaves from his leather pouch and stuffed them into a curved clay pipe. He lit the leaves with a flick of his finger, then began inhaling the smoke through his mouth and exhaling it through his ears. Finally, he nodded to indicate that the camp was pitched to his satisfaction, and ambled into his tent.

Urrn spread blankets made from woven strips of furry yellow hide onto the ground outside of their new overlord's tent. Even though it was still daytime, Mayberry and Marshall collapsed onto the hides, lying next to each other in an awkward heap.

Urrn dug into a soft brown animal-bladder sack and withdrew a gray, gooey-looking ball. He ripped off a piece with his thumb and forefinger, tossed it into his mouth, and began to chew.

Mayberry's and Marshall's bodies went rigid. They both bolted up. *Food.*

He took two more dough balls from the sack and handed them to the newcomers. Marshall's was green, Mayberry's orange. Urrn used his back molars to chomp into his ball, chewing just a few times before swallowing.

"Good," he grunted.

Mayberry was startled and looked over at Marshall, who raised his eyebrows in wonder.

"You speak English," Marshall confirmed to Urrn.

Urrn grunted tersely and tore off another piece of food.

Mayberry and Marshall exchanged glances. Until now, Urrn had communicated solely with grunts or hand signals. This was a small improvement, but he still didn't seem ready to freely communicate.

Marshall held his sticky green ball and gave it a squeeze. He tore off a chunk with his teeth and rolled the chalky substance around his mouth. He was going to spit it into the dirt, but having something edible in his mouth triggered intense hunger pains. It seemed like the wrong time to contemplate whether or not it was safe to eat. He glanced over at Mayberry, who was sniffing her own meal suspiciously.

Marshall chewed until his jaw ached, but it was hard to break the tough substance down into pieces that were small enough to swallow. The unfamiliar taste of fermented milk and rotting grain made his stomach roil, so he forced himself to swallow a few of the smaller pieces whole. It wasn't *that* bad. Some people on Earth considered fried insects, raw fish, and animal organs to be delicacies, so eating this—whatever it was—couldn't be *that* much worse. Or maybe it could.

Mayberry, who hadn't taken a bite yet, looked like she barely had enough energy left to laugh, but she did.

"What?"

"You look like you're eating a live mouse."

"A live mouse might taste better than this. Urrn, is this the only food you have?"

"It's very filling and nutritious," Urrn declared, devouring another mouthful.

Progress, Marshall thought.

"What is it?"

Urrn didn't respond, but at least he was starting to communicate.

Meanwhile, if they had to eat raw putty, they'd eat raw putty.

They were lucky to be alive. He finished eating his ball. Mayberry steadily ate small pieces of her orange ball until the whole thing was gone.

After finishing, she cleared her throat and scooted over to Urrn. "How long have you been . . . here?" Mayberry asked. "Are there other people here, too?"

Urrn slowly lifted up his head and responded, his face blank. "I've never seen other humans before," he said in a monotone. "I've been here for many, *many* years, but don't know *where* we are."

"Well, you must be from Earth," Marshall exclaimed. "You're human. And you speak English."

Urrn looked up at the sky for a minute, thinking hard, then dropped his head and went mute.

"Okay," Marshall interjected gently, trying a different tack. "I wonder what the inhabitants call this world."

Urrn took a few seconds before mumbling "Nith" into his knees.

"Nith?" Marshall said encouragingly.

"It means . . . something like . . . Earth."

"Can you speak Monga's language?" Mayberry asked.

"Our vocal cords aren't built for that." Urrn seemed to be growing more comfortable conversing with them, for now. "I taught him enough English for us to communicate. On Earth, my name sounds different, but on his tongue it is pronounced Urrn. You can call me that too."

Mayberry touched Urrn's shoulder softly. "Have you ever tried to get home?"

Urrn hunched down and backed away from Mayberry, then rose and walked briskly away. *Urrn's will has been broken, and now he's a slave trapped in a living hell,* Marshall thought. He swore to himself that he'd jump off the cliff with Mayberry in tow before becoming a zombie like Urrn.

CHAPTER 30

THE NEXT MORNING, Urrn tended to the crude
metal pan, holding it steadily over the campfire's
open flame. Breakfast was made from the same
dough balls, this time pounded flat with a wooden mallet, torn
into narrow strips, and fried in animal fat. It was crisp and
easier to chew, and the flavor was somewhat less loathsome.

Monga exited his tent, stretched all his arms out, scratched
his belly with four hands, and then trotted over to them just as
they finished their meal.

"Teech keedluns magik," he announced with a casual wave
of his hands.

Mayberry was pleasantly surprised by his declaration, but
she had no idea how much instruction they'd need before having a fighting chance to escape. Of course, she was happy to

take advantage of every opportunity Monga offered to teach her how to summon her powers.

Monga pushed out his chest and pounded it with his fists. "Keedluns bettr if yu magik. Magik, hep Monga."

"Yes, Monga. That's what we're *all* about. Learning how to do magic to help *you*," she responded. The sarcasm dripping from her voice was beyond Monga's tenuous understanding of the human language.

Monga took them to an open meadow nearby. He started the lessons by uttering what sounded like "Loofackle," then demonstrating a quick gesture with his fingers to move and direct small objects, like pebbles and sticks. Then he waved a hand to indicate that Marshall should use the spell to lift a small pile of dirt.

Marshall did his best to mimic the word Monga had used, along with the corkscrewing finger motion with his right fingers. The dust on top of the pile dimpled slightly, as if a raindrop had struck, but nothing else happened.

Monga swatted the back of Marshall's head with one of his tails.

"Hey!" Marshall yelped, bringing his hand to his head, then looking at the trace of blood on his fingers.

"Keedlun no lerrn," Monga said, shaking his head in disapproval.

"He's trying, Monga," said Mayberry plaintively.

Monga crossed his sets of arms. "Try mo."

Then Monga crooked a finger at Mayberry.

"Keedlun do. *Do.*"

Mayberry closed her eyes to focus, then opened them, chanted the mysterious word, and moved her fingers the way Monga had showed them.

A soft white glow formed around her fingers, then bolted into the pile, blasting it into a dust cloud that spun lazily in a clockwise circle before floating to the ground. Mayberry was dumbstruck. She'd actually done a spell . . . and without the compelling motivation of fighting for her life.

"Mo bettr," Monga decreed, flicking his tail in the dust next to Marshall's legs, making him jump to attention.

Marshall had a clearer idea of how to sound out the chant after hearing Mayberry do it, so he concentrated harder and tried again with the accompanying movement. A dim white light flared from his fingers, and his dirt formed a loose sloppy oval in the air before falling to the ground, looking exactly the same as all the other debris.

"I *did* it," he shouted happily to Mayberry. "Can you believe it?"

"Mo bettr," Monga said, ignoring the self-congratulation. "Do mo."

CHAPTER 31

F OR THE NEXT FEW DAYS, Monga drilled them as
relentlessly as Navy SEAL trainees.

First, he taught them how to do simple power
spells that required only a word and gesture. The specific
words necessary to cast a spell never meant anything to Marshall, but during the third day of training, he discovered that
he didn't need to vocalize the words to cast spells, as long as
he *thought* them clearly while performing the correct gestures.
The necessary gestures weren't hard to master, only requiring
their fingers to be splayed, pressed together, or fisted, then
moved at the right pace in the right direction.

When he cast a spell the right way, he could feel the energy zap into his body and then coalesce in his fingers. He saw
that many of the spells' colors and characteristics mirrored
those of the basic elements. Fire spells were red, water blue,

wind gray, and earth brown. Basic kinetic energy power spells were usually bright white.

They mastered the beginning lessons so quickly that Monga soon moved them up to more complicated conjuring. The most powerful spells involved more difficult words, intricate gestures, and occasionally whole-body movements that reminded Marshall of modern dance.

Before long, he could use power spells to lift and direct objects as heavy as boulders or big as trees, brown earth spells to create fissures in the ground or cause earthquakes, gray wind spells to manipulate the air or create small tornadoes to blow objects apart, or blue water spells to conjure giant floating whirlpools or spit torrents of water. With a thought and the flick of an index finger, he could summon a red fire spell, which created a tiny flame that—with another thought—shot from his fingers and exploded into a stream of fire that engulfed the target he aimed for.

Each day it became easier for Marshall to remember new spells. It was as if his DNA had been programmed to do magic, the way babies are wired to crawl, walk, and babble. Monga's demands rose with each increase in their skill. He indicated his displeasure for even the slightest of errors with gruff words or flicks of the tail.

Mayberry's spells were more naturally beautiful and perfectly formed than Marshall's. It was amazing to see how her artistic talent flowered, even in the most difficult of times.

One day before breakfast, Marshall saw that Mayberry

had woven some flowers into her hair and stuffed her pockets with leaves and grass.

"Marshall, I have a hunch that Nith's organic elements can increase our powers—just the way the feathers did."

She was absolutely right, and they immediately saw the effects of their spells increase. That night they braided bits of wood, grass and bones into their hair, made bracelets of fur, and used the hole-punch on Marshall's pocketknife to drill through soft stones, which they strung and wore as pendants. They offered one to Urrn, who nodded and put it around his neck. The next morning in the bright sunlight, they all looked like Lost Boys from *Peter Pan*.

The combination of intense focus, exercise, sunshine, and protein-packed dough balls were making Marshall and Mayberry mentally tougher and physically stronger. The days and nights started to blend into each other, so Marshall decided to keep track of time by carving a hash mark for every day on a stick. He stored it in his backpack.

The next morning at breakfast, Mayberry looked at Urrn, who was feeding innards from one of Monga's recent kills to his pet. "Do *you* think we'll ever see our parents again?"

Urrn ignored her question.

Mayberry rested her head on Marshall's shoulder, and he put his arm around her waist and tilted his head against hers. Marshall detested being enslaved on Nith just as much as Mayberry. The good news was that he *had* saved her life more than once. He *did* occasionally catch her looking at him in a new way. If they ever got home, things might be different between them.

After each day's harsh regime of magical training, avoiding Monga's wrath, and completing various backbreaking camp chores, Marshall was exhausted. The nights were chilly, but thankfully, not as cold as autumn in Minnesota. Marshall and Mayberry had new mats Urrn had taught them to weave out of jungle vines, and covered themselves with the yellow animal fur blankets that Urrn had given them.

CHAPTER 32

DURING AN ESPECIALLY GRUELING training session, Monga demanded that Mayberry hold a heavy mass of swirling water in place fifty feet up in the air. She lost her focus for a second, the water spell broke, and the cold water pelted down, soaking them all to the bone.

"We all needed a good shower," Marshall said laughing, pointing at the dirt turned muddy on his clothes, then nodding at Monga's dripping fur. Monga hated getting wet and always went into his tent at the first sign of a drizzle.

Enraged by the water covering his precious fur, Monga whirled his fingers and muttered for at least ten seconds. A sparking ball of yellow coalesced in his palm and divided into two marble-size yellow comets, which shot toward Mayberry and Marshall. Like guided missiles, they swooped around the humans' backs and splashed into their marks.

In an instant, they had both crumpled into the grass, reduced to whimpering puddles of agony, while Urrn crouched
nearby, patting Uuth's head. The pain spread into Marshall's
eyes—it felt like a bag of pins was being driven into them—
but he dimly managed to perceive a blurry shadow jumping
in front of Monga.

"Monga, stop!" Urrn shouted.

Marshall gasped in relief as the burning eased and his
eyes regained their ability to focus. Monga was staring intently
at his empty fingers, clearly surprised—Urrn's intervention
made him lose his concentration.

Monga's lips drew away from his teeth to roar out a pain
spell, and his fingers flashed over and over until a bright yellow fireball rotated in his palm. He unleashed it on Urrn.

After it struck its mark, it was glowing so hot that Marshall could feel the heat radiating from Urrn's back. The intensity of the pain knocked Urrn to the ground. Then Monga
stepped in and started whipping him bloody with the tips of
his tails.

Marshall sprang to his feet. If Monga didn't stop, he was
going to kill Urrn. Mayberry appeared at Marshall's side, and
together they conjured white power spells that began to glow
on their fingertips.

"Stop, Monga, stop," Mayberry screamed, clearly prepared
to attack Monga if she had to.

Monga looked into the determined faces of the two humans—and at their fingers, poised to fire power at him. His

body sagged and he released the pain spell. His purple eyes narrowed, and he shook his head violently, as if trying to deny the fact that Marshall and Mayberry had threatened him with the magic *he* had taught them. He stomped his hooves in the dust, dropped his head, then headed for the solitude of his tent.

Marshall and Mayberry reached down to help Urrn to his feet, drawing his arms around their shoulders so they could help him hobble over to his mat by their campsite.

"Thank you," Urrn croaked as he lay down and curled into a fetal position. "He was going to kill me."

"No, thank *you*," Mayberry said, sitting by Urrn's head while Marshall sat by his feet, patting his leg tentatively. They stayed with him until Urrn fell asleep.

Later, at dinnertime, Urrn staggered up off his mat to join their meal. They all sat silently, listening to the noises in the forest around them, until suddenly Urrn blurted out, "I don't know what you did to deserve being exiled here like me, but I'm going to help you escape anyway."

Puzzled, Marshall and Mayberry looked at each other. For now, it seemed better not to question their only ally's motivation too closely.

"Teech keedluns magik."

CHAPTER 33

A S MAYBERRY STARTED drifting to sleep, she imagined her mother's voice floating down the hall outside her bedroom, the smell of her father's after-shave, and the feeling of warmth from the old cast-iron radiator in her bedroom. She knew, though, that these thoughts didn't reflect reality. The voice was the faint roar of the river drifting up the canyon, the smell the fragrance of native plants carried on the night breeze, and the warmth the pocket of air created by her body and the insulating yellow blanket.

There was, however, a pleasant buzzing that wasn't a fig-ment of her imagination. She lifted her head, rubbed her eyes, and peered around. Marshall slept a few feet away, breath-ing heavily, while Urrn snored nearby. Then she saw a plump furry brown creature ambling toward her on all fours through the darkness. It had intelligent-looking oval eyes, a moist black snout, long pointy ears, and a fluffy curved tail that sprouted from its neck instead of its bottom. It loped over and nuzzled Mayberry's cheek, purring like a cat. It leaned back, and as its eyes stared into hers, a pulse of warm, relaxing energy flooded her mind, giving Mayberry a deep sense of calm.

She reached out to stroke the creature, and as soon as her hand made contact, a sound came to her mind . . . *Co-Co. Your name is Co-Co.* When she thought the name, the creature whirled joyfully and purred louder. The little animal faced her and began to mimic her every move like a mirror puppet. When she laughed at the performance, Co-Co responded with a contented whistling. Mayberry had no idea how such a small, gentle creature, who looked totally defenseless, could survive for even a day on this scary planet. Co-Co hopped in close to cuddle against Mayberry's legs, so she laid her head back down and gathered the furry body to her chest like she had her teddy bear when she was a small child. Co-Co radiated enough heat to dispel the night chill. With her new pet nestled beside her, Mayberry slept deeper and better than she had in years.

Monga didn't seem surprised or upset to see Co-Co riding Mayberry's shoulder the next morning. Perhaps interspecies bonding wasn't unusual in Nith. After all, Urrn had Uuth.

CHAPTER 34

◦━━━━▽━━━━◦

MARSHALL WAS HAPPY to encounter another friendly Nith creature, and Co-Co gave him a friendly snuggle before returning to Mayberry's arms.

After that day's magic lesson, Mayberry had an idea. She'd seen some grasses with fine, grain-like tips growing near the clearing, and Urrn had mentioned that they were edible. Monga kept a sweet-smelling, honey-scented sap in a heavy clay pot outside his tent, but Mayberry knew he would notice if even the tiniest bit was missing, so she harvested some sweet brown berries along with her grass.

She ground the tips, used water and berries to create a soft mush, then shaped the rough dough into patties that resembled her chocolate chip cookies, with the tiny brown berries standing in for chips.

She put Urrn's metal pan inside a crude mud oven to bake her mishmash mélange. She wasn't sure if the results of her experiment would be edible, but when she plucked the cookies out of the oven, they smelled surprisingly good. She tore off a warm piece and popped it into her mouth. The flavor of Nith cookies was unclassifiable by Earth standards, but they still tasted way better than anything she'd eaten here.

Marshall strolled over and evaluated the pan of cookies, eventually choosing one with crispy edges, while Urrn watched and Uuth slavered, pulling at his leash. Marshall took a tentative bite, smacked his lips, and wolfed the whole thing down. Mayberry nodded for him to take another, which he ate a bit more slowly this time, a look of near rapture on his face.

Urrn gingerly picked up a cookie from the pan, holding it as delicately as if it were a priceless Ming dynasty vase. He lowered himself onto a tree stump and took a bite.

"Good," he said, beaming at Mayberry. He tossed a large crumb into Uuth's gaping mouth, and the faithful pet nearly danced in delight.

"Thank you, Mayberry," Marshall said. "These are amazing. A week ago, we were the Sleviccs' captives, about to become human barbecue, and now we're . . . well, we're still captives . . . but at least we're learning magic and eating cookies."

Urrn wiped his hands on his rough leather pants and looked up pensively. "The Sleviccs wouldn't have *eaten* you. Why did you think that?"

"Because they were roasting a pig-looking animal on a spit, and they had a couple more on tap in a cage," Mayberry said. "They locked us up in a hut right next to the live ones."

Urrn shook his head and sighed. "Those were Varnets. They're very bad animals—worse than hyenas and harder to catch—but they're tasty, kinda like a cross between pork and chicken. Isolated Varnets are harmless, but when they form packs, they swarm and take down any vulnerable prey in their path.

"Sleviccs *like* humans. I'd been living with them for years when Monga captured me. You must have seen all the artifacts the Sleviccs have collected from human visitors over the centuries."

Mayberry was stunned. "So why would the Sleviccs lock us up and light a huge bonfire? And start floating around it before they ate dinner?"

"I know what happened," Urrn said, shaking his head. "Once a year, when the three moons align, the Slevicc tribes meditate and pray together, as a way to thank the gods for creating and protecting them. The elders probably locked you away to make sure you didn't interrupt the ceremony. They believe that breaking even one Slevicc's trance before the ceremony is completed would cause years of bad luck. They tried to chase you down when they realized you were missing to help you . . . They know how dangerous Nith is . . . and they hate Monga."

Mayberry was flabbergasted. Marshall sat down heavily

beside her and put his face in his hands. Lost in thought, Mayberry started handing out the remaining cookies from the metal pan. She gave one to Marshall and two more to Urrn.

Urrn sniffed the cookie before cramming it into his mouth. As he chewed, his forehead wrinkled and his eyes pooled with tears. "Cookies remind me of home," he said softly. "When I first got here, I'd open my eyes every morning and pray that I was back home. But I never was, because I deserve this."

Mayberry was at a loss for words. What could he have done to deserve *this*? "Did you try to get home?"

Ignoring Mayberry's question, he squeezed his eyes shut and started to rock himself back and forth. "We used to play together in the snow, then Mom would make us hot cocoa and brownies."

He slowly opened his eyes, which locked on the remnant of the cookie in his palm. Then, finishing the last bite, he dusted a few crumbs off his clothes, rose, and walked away.

She turned to face Marshall. "What *happened* to him?"

Marshall pursed his lips and rolled his shoulders forward. "I have no idea, but I'm guessing that we'll find out eventually."

CHAPTER 35

AFTER FIVE MORE DAYS of training, Monga wanted his pupils to demonstrate their repertoire of magic spells. He moved from the practice field to the nearby cliff overlooking the river.

Monga lifted his chin and grunted in Marshall's direction. "Yu uman first."

Marshall took a few steps forward, close enough to catch a whiff of Monga's musty fur. He leaned in and stretched out his hands to cast a wind spell. His fingers lit up, and he quickly drew what looked like a soft gray spiderweb in the air, then blew the threads away. A powerful gust of air rose, carrying the camp's firewood stack up into the air before turning it into a wild tornado of wood that spiraled into the sky. Marshall crooked a finger at the wood, which dropped obediently back into its triangular stack near Monga's feet.

Monga snorted his approval. "Goot." Then he raised one of his upper arms and pointed at Mayberry.

Mayberry remained in place, thrusting out her hands. She hummed a tune under her breath, and white miasma ripped from her fingers. She traced a pattern of waves into the air, and suddenly the firewood leaped from the ground and began spinning like a propeller, creating an impassable wooden force field. After she twisted her fingers clockwise, each piece of firewood zoomed straight down into the earth, forming a perfectly spaced wooden fence around the camp's northern perimeter. Then Mayberry spun her index finger counter-clockwise, making a small red flame appear at its tip. With a flick of her wrist, she transformed the flame into a towering pillar of fire that whooshed fifty feet into the air. She turned to Marshall with a satisfied *match that* look.

Marshall narrowed his eyes and rapidly moved his now-bluish fingers in the air. A giant waterspout materialized and began pelting Mayberry's fire with shots of water that flicked at it from every direction, throwing punches like a champion boxer. The fire spell resisted the attack, ducking and dodging the piston blows of water while making defiant hissing noises. Still, soon its volume was greatly reduced, and eventually the fire spell succumbed. Wheezing, it extinguished.

"Is goot, is goot. Keedluns reddy."

"Ready. Ready for what?" Marshall asked.

"Keedluns hep Monga geet steeck, den keel Olathe, den tek all." Monga drew a finger across his throat and pointed to a range of mountain peaks on the western horizon. "Go dere, keel Olathe."

"What stick? Do what? Who is Olathe?" Marshall asked, hoping he had misunderstood what Monga was saying. Clouds of smoke hovered over the angry-looking mountains.

"Olathe is Monga's brother," Urrn interjected. "He wants us to help him kill his older brother."

"Why do you want to keel . . . um . . . kill him?" Mayberry asked Monga.

"Olathe kep mates. Now Monga keel Olathe with steeck, tek mates. Den tek Nith," Monga answered with a confident nod.

That night after dinner, Marshall, Mayberry, and Urrn sat by the waning campfire to discuss Monga's pronouncement.

Urrn opened the discussion. "Monga's taught me magic for years, and during the whole time, he's been constantly searching this area for more humans, which he needs so he can get the 'stick.' Now I know why. Monga's afraid of Olathe because Olathe is more powerful. He must be because he stole Monga's wives and kept them. Monga thinks if he gets the 'stick,' whatever that is, it will help him kill Olathe."

"What a mess," Marshall said, shaking his head. "I can't believe that we're going to be risking our lives because of Monga's girl problems."

"I can't imagine why he has girl problems," Mayberry replied. "He's such a charmer. I bet Olathe is, too. But seriously, I think he's also saying that he wants us to help him conquer this whole world after he gets his wives back?"

"That's what it sounded like," Marshall said, throwing a piece of wood in the fire. "Urrn, do you think we have a chance of getting out of this in one piece?"

Urrn shook his head soberly and stared into the fire. "Probably not."

"I doubt it, too," Mayberry chimed in. "Monga taught us magic so we could fight for him. He doesn't care if we live or die, as long as we help him get what he wants."

"That might be true, but Monga's marked us, which means that—at least for now—we have to do what he wants. We can't beat him," Urrn said with finality.

Mayberry instinctively reached a hand back to rub her mark.

"We need to escape before he takes us into those mountains," Marshall said, sighing as he pulled the shabby fur blanket up around his shoulders.

"Yap," she agreed, and then winced. "I mean, yes. We have to make our move as soon as we can."

Urrn looked concerned, but he still nodded his assent. "How will we know when the time to chance a fight with him is right? We need a plan."

The three of them moved their heads together with their backs facing Monga's tent and started whispering.

CHAPTER 36

THE AIR THE NEXT MORNING was cold and brittle, and an odd, cloying scent drifted past. The sun, muted under dense gray cloud cover, looked more like a distant street lamp than a viable source of heat.

To encourage his protégées to get serious about packing up and preparing for what was coming, Monga stomped his hooves ferociously while shouting unintelligible orders.

Mayberry, Marshall, and Urrn all labored with brisk efficiency, using various spells to speed up the process. Co-Co padded around, happily following in Mayberry's footsteps. The camp was dismantled in no time, the bundles were neatly tied on Uuth's back, and almost too soon, they were ready to go.

Monga started shuffling down the river trail. After an hour of leading his slaves on a fast-paced hike, he turned onto a muddy path that passed through a forest of squat, smoke-gray trees. The trees had spiky branches that flowed down to the ground and fought for space, like rolls of twisted barbed wire. Spindly plants filled in the gaps. Without the narrow space created by the trail, the thicket would be impassable.

As the sunlight faded, an energetic Monga and the panting hikers exited the dense forest. With the woods behind them now, they stopped to pitch camp on an open meadow that faced a vista of rolling hills. Herds of mammoth-size creatures grazed in the distance.

"Should we be worried about those?" Mayberry asked Urrn, pointing to the nearest herd.

"They won't bother us," Urrn said. "They're herbivores—not aggressive at all. You'll see tomorrow. There are packs of two-headed carnivores that can bring down beasts even as large as those, but they hunt at night and try to avoid Monga's kind."

Mayberry shrugged off the heavy bundle she'd been carrying. The uneven weight of her burden wasn't easy to balance, nor were her body's muscles accustomed to hauling such a heavy load. Casting spells required continuous focus, so magic only worked in short bursts for physical tasks; she couldn't just levitate her pack and keep it floating next to her all day. She watched Marshall massaging the tender spots on his own shoulder blades.

"I'll do yours if you do mine," she suggested.

Marshall's eyes closed in relief. "That works. Who goes first?"

"It was my idea, so me first," she said, smiling and presenting her back to him.

"You stink," Marshall said, placing his hands on her shoulders, then quickly drawing them off.

She grinned. "I know, but I haven't had a real bath in . . . like, since before we got here."

"That's not what I meant—but actually, right now we both smell," he said. "This may hurt you . . . I mean . . . touching Monga's mark."

She sighed and her head slumped forward. "Can we just try for a second? I'm desperate, and those mountains look just as far away as they did when we started hiking."

"Fine," he said starting to knead her shoulders with strong hands. "That okay?"

Mayberry hummed her assent, and Co-Co ran to jump into her lap and started purring. She gently said, "We hiked on the trail all day."

"True, but we had to stay on the trail to get through the forest," he pointed out. "From here we can go cross-country in any direction Monga wants. And we have no idea where that precious stick is."

Urrn met Marshall's quizzical look and shook his head no. "I've heard that it *exists*, but that's about it."

After a blissful interval, Marshall patted her shoulders one last time, then stopped. Mayberry stretched out her arms out and stood up. Her lower back and hips were still sore, but her upper back felt much looser. She shifted behind Marshall and pulled down his hoodie, then started massaging his shoulders. They were broader and stronger than she'd expected, and she had to work hard to break up the tense muscle.

"That's *good*," he muttered happily, slowly expelling his breath.

The next morning, Monga set a brisk pace straight into the forest. Flocks of low-flying birdlike creatures zipped past them, while a red, leather-winged beast almost as large as a pterodactyl soared through the gray clouds. It banked sharply above them, then swooped down, leading with its yard-long, needle-sharp yellow beak. Before it could attack, its keen eyes spotted the red luminescence forming on Monga's beefy fingers, at which point it darted away, keening.

They walked between scattered herds of herbivores with heads as big as small cars, resting on bodies as big as garbage trucks that made the heads look small by comparison. The creatures ignored them, grazing on grass, raising their heads to pluck branches from thorny bushes, or stomping down trees with their massive legs so they could gnaw on the branches.

That evening, as they rested, plump, hamster-size critters with glowing red eyes skittered around at the perimeter of their campsite. Periodically, many-legged wolverine sized creatures dashed in from the shadows and swallowed the red-eyed beasties whole before bolting away from the light cast by the campfire.

Mayberry stroked Co-Co's fur and tried to ignore the hungry predators.

CHAPTER 37

THE NEXT DAY, as they approached a deep clump of thorny bushes, Co-Co started chittering excitedly. In two lightning-fast kangaroo hops, she positioned herself directly in front of Mayberry. A venom-dripping stinger popped out of her tail, which whipped forward like a scorpion's, poised to strike. Uuth loosed a low nasal grunt and took a few steps backward, wiggling the spiky ball at the end of his tail. They both were ready for action.

Monga turned his head to see what was causing the commotion. Just as he did, a two-headed beast with copper-colored scales leaped from the bushes, nearly landing on top of Marshall. Its long ears flattened, the deep black pupils in its four yellow eyes widened, and its massive jaws opened, revealing vicious rows of curved teeth.

Marshall went statue-still as his fingers started to glow

white. Instead of attacking, though, the creature flicked out two thick, moist yellow tongues and licked Marshall's face like a happy dog, leaving behind a thin layer of goo.

"*Don't move,*" Marshall screamed to Mayberry, whose fingers had lit up with red miasma. "His name is Mirrt." He reached out to pat the beast, who lowered his heads to give Marshall easier access. After receiving a few more encouraging pats, he rewarded Marshall with sloppy licks to the face. For a few seconds, Marshall's mind was flooded with flashing lights and bright colors, and then his core flooded with warmth. His own familiar had arrived at last, bringing the boldness and confidence he'd always wished for.

Monga sniffed disgustedly and turned away. Mayberry strolled over to welcome Mirrt, who seemed excited to join his new family.

They started walking again. By later that afternoon, they'd left the grassy hills behind and entered a narrow canyon, its steep walls glistening with crystalline veins of purple, green, and dusty rose quartz. The canyon became wider as they penetrated farther into it, and it finally flattened out into a broad, rock-covered desert valley.

In the distance, Marshall saw a gleaming temple with a Byzantine-style domed roof. The edifice was set on a stone island in the middle of a glistening pool of dark blue water, peppered by brown rocks and surrounded by trees. The bright midday sun shimmered off the stark white building. A hundred feet beyond was a wide ribbon of placid water. It was broad and slow, which meant that it wasn't the river they'd been looking for.

"Hurrey, yu." Monga's voice rumbled with palpable excitement. He fast-trotted in a circle around them, loudly smacking his four hands together. "Mak fastre."

As they got closer to the oasis, Marshall was amazed by the stately temple and its surroundings. The "trees" weren't trees at all, but massive pillars carved from the same green crystal he'd seen embedded in the canyon walls. Their apexes blossomed into long, twisted spikes that spread out like palm leaves. Over forty of the pillars were perfectly spaced around the circular pond. The structure covering the island was a wondrous architectural feat, whose elegance matched that of ancient Greek temples. Columns flared up to sculpted cornices that supported the red-tiled dome; the peak of the whole edifice soared elegantly at least sixty feet above the ground. A bluish-gray stone staircase encased its entire elevated base.

"What is this place?" Marshall stuttered, astonished.

"I have no idea," Urrn replied quietly, perplexed. "I've never been here."

"Innit steeck. Ya, innit steeck," Monga proclaimed, clapping his four hands excitedly. "Soon wives."

CHAPTER 38

SEEMS LIKE A STRANGE PLACE to find a stick," Marshall said.

The familiars were agitated. Uuth stomped his feet, repeatedly smacked his spiked tail into the ground, and wouldn't move a step forward, in spite of Urrn's best efforts to coax him. Co-Co darted wildly back and forth in front of Mayberry with her stinger exposed, screeching. Mirrt bent into a low defensive crouch facing the water, like a lion on the prowl. His claws scraped deep lines in the earth. The low, emphatic buzzing noise in his mind told Marshall that Mirrt was warning him to back away.

Monga blithely ignored the familiars' erratic behavior and motioned the humans toward the stepping-stones in the water, making bouncing signals with his hands to indicate that they needed to traverse them to get to the temple.

Mayberry surveyed the curious stones, which were ridged like ancient ammonites. Even though their enormous size implied an equally enormous weight, they bobbed sedately in the water, drifting in a nearly imperceptible clockwise direction.

Monga stepped onto the nearest stone, as surefooted as a mountain goat. The stone wobbled and sank slightly under his weight, but didn't capsize.

"Com fasst," he ordered urgently, then jumped agilely onto the next stone, delicately juggling his bulk so that he didn't skid and fall into the water.

Urrn didn't stop to think. Leaving Uuth on the shore, he jumped aboard the closest stone, then took long agile leaps from stone to stone toward the temple.

Marshall halted at the pond's edge. He guessed the stones floated in their orderly pattern because they were tethered together below the surface of the murky water.

He jumped cautiously, balancing on the edge of the nearest stone. "It's easy," he said to Mayberry. "Just do it."

The stone rocked slightly beneath him. It felt like being on the deck of a big ship. There was a slight swaying, but no sense that he was about to be pitched overboard. Marshall boldly leaped onto a different nearby stone, then another and another. In less than thirty seconds, he was a third of the way to the temple. Monga was nearly there, and Urrn was close behind.

As he watched the two of them racing ahead, Marshall realized that the water beneath each stepping-stone that had been touched was beginning to bubble, and the bubbles were rapidly expanding into plumes of aerated fizz. Behind him, Mayberry was finally starting to amble her way across. She showed no sense of urgency as she jumped, and stopped on each rock to gawk at the beautiful scenery.

Like a missile launched from a nuclear submarine, a brown stepping-stone suddenly burst out of the water behind Mayberry. Before Marshall could process what was happening, the stone warped into a monster: a sharp-scaled purple beast zooming directly for the back of Mayberry's head. Her heightened senses must have warned her, because she immediately ducked, and Marshall heard a *whoosh* as the creature zipped by and its ugly toothy head plunged back into the water with a huge splash.

Before he and Mayberry could speak, another stepping-stone burst from the water with a loud sucking sound, targeting him this time. As soon as the words *get back* entered his mind, a power spell shot from his fingers, deflecting the stone-creature. Its wicked teeth clicked together on air as it ricocheted off another beast that had launched upward.

By now, every stepping-stone that had been touched by the travelers was sputtering to life. The idyllic scene became a chaotic pinball game, with the two humans remaining on the pond's surface serving as fragile glass balls being attacked by the steel ball defenders.

Without panicking, Marshall conjured the defensive spells he needed as the monsters swirled around him. He leaped, ducked, dodged, and swerved while deflecting the barrage of stone-beasts cascading toward him and Mayberry. Zigzagging from stone to stone, he finally leaped off the final rock and onto the temple steps just as a stone-beast reached the spot he'd just left.

He collapsed on the steps, panting, and then wheeled to find Mayberry. A humongous stone-beast was speeding toward her, with its fang-filled mouth agape.

As soon as her foot touched the next stone, it burst up and rocketed her twenty feet straight up into the air. She somehow managed to balance on the creature's back with her legs clutching its sides like a rodeo bull rider. The other beast targeting her raced past and twisted its massive head, trying to chomp into her flesh, but instead flew harmlessly beneath her new mount, which dodged right to protect its prize.

The stone-beast she was riding shook wildly, trying to turn its head far enough to bite into Mayberry's body, but before it could, it fell back down into the pond. A huge jet of water splashed up as the beast's body pierced the pond's surface, and both rider and mount vanished.

Stunned, Marshall clamped his hands to his head in dismay, but milliseconds later, Mayberry spurted up out of the gusher. She landed feet first on a stone that was just sputtering to life, but skipped off into a forward handspring so fast it seemed her feet had barely touched it.

She stuck the perfect landing on the temple's steps, soaked but unscathed.

CHAPTER 39

WHEN MAYBERRY'S FEET touched the stone steps, it was as if a giant off switch had been hit, turning the living beasts back into rock. They plummeted into the water, pockmarking the pond with a series of huge splashes.

"How did you do that?" Marshall asked breathlessly.

"No idea," she replied, her lungs still sucking for air.

A sharp snort broke her out of her thank-God-I'm-alive moment. It was Monga, pacing in an agitated circle. He was stopping at the same place again and again before continuing his rounds. Mayberry and Marshall followed his gaze toward the temple. From shore, the space between the building's tall white columns had seemed to be open and unobstructed. Now Mayberry saw that a solid black wall filled each space between the columns. There was no visible entryway.

Marshall turned to address Mayberry, who was squeezing the water out of her vest. "Well, we barely survived *that*. I wonder what's next."

"Me too. I'm guessing that's where the stick is . . . I wonder how he thinks we're going to get inside."

Even though she was wet and cold, her unfathomable victory over the stone-beasts had left her adrenaline pumping— she felt nearly euphoric. When they reached the black wall, she rapped her knuckles gently on its surface, expecting the feel of stone or metal. Instead, it was smooth and rubbery.

"We opeen," Monga declared.

"We open," she repeated. "As in, *we*?"

"Yes. Yu, yu, yu," he said, pointing to each human in turn. "Opeen, geet steeck."

She watched, mesmerized, as Monga swept his fingers over the surface of the featureless black wall. One of his lower hands touched something and froze.

"Hans giv," he ordered.

"Hands?" Marshall repeated in surprise.

Monga impatiently grabbed Marshall's hand, nearly jerking Marshall off his feet as he pulled him forward and pressed his hand against the wall.

As Monga fit Marshall's hand into the impression, Marshall turned to Mayberry. "This indentation had to have been made by a human hand—he's putting my five fingers and palm into an imprint."

"Do you think your hand is part of a key or something?"

"Something. It felt pretty solid when I first put my hand on it, but now I can push into it a little, like clay. It's getting sort of warm and tingly, too."

Monga guided Marshall's right hand into another indentation on the wall, parallel with the left.

"Marcha, stey. Maybear, Urrn, com."

Mayberry followed Monga as he clomped around the curved black wall. At another location between the pillars, he stopped and felt around on the black wall.

"Han."

She reached out, and Monga's giant hand pushed her small left hand into an indentation. She could feel the spaces for four fingers and a thumb, in exactly the right proportions, so she slid her right hand over the wall and found the other spot easily enough.

"Maybear, stey," Monga said, trotting off with Urrn in tow.

Moments later, she heard his booming voice echoing from the other side of the temple, rhythmically chanting in his language. A spurt of kinetic energy sprang into her hands and rolled through her body. She struggled to keep her body upright and her hands firmly in place. *It's a good thing I'm leaning in against the wall for support*, she thought, disoriented, *Because I'd fall without it being here.*

Monga's voice droned on. Finally, it stopped. "Hans off," he bellowed.

A rainbow of colors flowed from the wall's edges and undulated inward toward its center. *Wow, this is . . .*

But before she could finish her thought, the wall became translucent, then disappeared. She spotted Marshall, staring in astonishment with his hands still up but nothing to press against. Urrn was visible in the other quadrant, wearing a rapt expression.

Monga smiled and snapped his jaws energetically.

CHAPTER 40

○────▽────○

STEECK!" MONGA SCREAMED with unabashed joy, scampering headlong into the open atrium.

Mayberry followed him across the polished hardwood parquet floor toward a beautiful crystal obelisk that stood at the chamber's center. Monga paused and stopped a few feet in front of it, mesmerized. Milky drool dripped from his mouth, and his purple eyes bulged. Mayberry squinted into the cloudy depths of the obelisk.

Something was floating inside. An iron hammer—one that looked much too heavy to lift—was suspended in the crystal, its handle wrapped in intricately inscribed leather.

"It's Excalibur!" Marshall shouted as he stepped next to her.

"Excalibur? But Excalibur's a *sword*."

"Right. That's not a sword," Urrn said, stupefied. "It's a ring . . . no, not just a ring. Look, you can read what it is right there. It's the Seal of Solomon. The seal was supposed to give King Solomon power over demons and djinns, and the ability to talk to animals. It's one of the most sacred artifacts in—"

"You guys are mental," Mayberry interjected. "It's clearly a *hammer*." As she stared, the inscriptions on the hammer suddenly became perfectly clear to her. "Mjölnir," she read, struggling with the pronunciation. The text said it could knock down mountains and be thrown for miles and still return to the thrower's hand. Thor had wielded it against giants and monsters. "Dude, that is *definitely* Thor's hammer. The mighty Thor, like in the Marvel comics."

"Mayberry, you must be hallucinating," Marshall said. "I am telling you it's King Arthur's sword. It says so right there on the hilt," he insisted. "Look, the inscription is all about Camelot, Arthur, and Lancelot . . . It's all true."

"*Stee . . . eee . . . ck, stee . . . eee . . . ck,*" Monga trilled, as transfixed as if he were drugged. His head swayed back and forth as he stared blank eyed into the crystal.

Perhaps there were mirrors inside the crystal that partitioned the obelisk, and they were each looking at the reflection of different objects. Mayberry slid over to see the view from Urrn's vantage point, but kept seeing the hammer . . . or, wait a minute, could it be a sword?

A deep velvety voice touched her mind, saying, "*The objects you see were once a part of me. I am also in the mind of Four-hands. He dreams of vengeance, conquest, and riches—greed is paralyzing his will. You, however, are speckled with light. If you act now, you can accept the object and its power before the dark one does."*

Mayberry's hand moved involuntarily toward the obelisk, driven by a will of its own. Her hand punctured the surface, and she was instantly sucked inside.

Time stopped.

Floating between earth and sky, she was bound by neither. Everyone outside the obelisk had been frozen in an immobile tableau. The obelisk's inner chamber was enormous, many times as big as it seemed from outside. She peered up through the obelisk's transparent walls to study the temple's arched ceiling. It was decorated with mosaics that depicted images of centaurs, hydras, harpies, and other mythological beings she recognized, but most of the art represented creatures and objects she'd never seen before. The artists' reverence for their subjects shone through the work. The temple was a cathedral, built by worshipful followers for the purpose of honoring a higher power.

Suddenly, a beam of light enveloped an object and floated it in front of Mayberry.

For a moment she saw a sword—Marshall's Excalibur—and was able to read the same description of Camelot that he'd seen.

Then the object transformed. It was a spinning ring of brass and iron, slightly tarnished and very old, set with four square-cut red stones. The Seal of Solomon.

She blinked, and it was the Cup of Jamshid, a Persian chalice in which the whole world was reflected.

It was the Bone of Ullr, upon which thousands of powerful incantations were carved.

It was Merlin's wand.

It was the Smoking Mirror that Tezcatlitopa used to view the universe.

It was Mercury's caduceus, then the Yata no Kagami, a sacred relic of Japanese myth.

And then, as it transformed again and again with every beat of her heart, she could sense only words like *Sampo* and *Amenonuhoko* and *Vitthakalai* and *Draupnir*.

All these objects flashed by at warp speed. Without comprehending the reason, she understood that she was seeing an infinite number of mystical artifacts from Earth and even other worlds.

The velvety voice spoke again. *"These objects of power have all existed somewhere in time and space. Your mind will select the object that is most suitable for you. After it does, your spirit will be free to determine its own path."*

Suddenly the sole object floating in front of her was an unadorned wooden wand. The dark brown wood tapered at each end, and a slight kink kept it from being perfectly straight. Although it appeared to be as inconsequential as an average stick lying on a forest floor, Mayberry recognized it at once as Merlin's wand. She reached her hand out, then felt a tremendous surge of adrenaline as her fingers made contact. Ancient druidic runes outlined in yellow light began to glow on its base. The wand told her that it could multiply the power of the wielder's spells, teach her new spells, or even be used to suck the life force from its target.

Suddenly she knew she'd be able to return to Nith. Time unfroze. The room sprang back to life.

CHAPTER 41

MONGA BOLTED FORWARD, reaching his upper hands toward the object of his desire, but his knuckles rebounded off the rock-hard crystal. The interior of the obelisk was empty. He turned to find Mayberry behind him, and the realization that another was holding the stick he had yearned to possess for so many years made him rear up on his hind legs and expel a deafening roar of anger and frustration. His two upper hands drew his swords, and his lower ones grabbed his daggers.

"Giv steeck!" he roared, his dark volcanic expression making it clear he was prepared to kill Mayberry if she didn't instantly comply.

Mayberry instinctively knew that the wand's extra power gave her the opportunity they'd been waiting for—a chance to defeat Monga. She had only seconds to strike, not enough time to let the wand teach her new spells, so she decided to keep it simple by allowing it to magnify the power of the spells she already knew. The wand's energy coursed through her body, making her feel invincible.

"I am going to give you exactly what you deserve, slave master," she snarled at Monga.

Game on.

Mayberry cast the first spell that popped into her mind, a power spell. The twisting pulse of bright, magnified power erupted from the tip of the wand and struck a hammer blow to the center of Monga's chest, blowing him backward. Flailing wildly for purchase, he careened headfirst into a stone column with a force so great that his swords flew from his hands.

"Awesome, Mayberry!" Marshall croaked, elated.

Urrn, following the plan they had agreed to around the campfire, separated from the two of them and shuffled over to the far wall, way out of Monga's line of sight.

Before Monga could recover, Mayberry's violent gray wind spell created a tornado that picked him up, whirled him in circles, then slammed his body into another stone column. When the wind spell finally released him, Monga crashed to the ground, groaning and madly bicycling his hooves.

Although clearly in pain, Monga still managed to regain his footing. His nose was broken, and his body was covered with quickly swelling bruises and wounds. Ignoring serious injuries that would have crippled or killed a human, Monga hurled a powerful white counterspell at Mayberry.

Mayberry cast the first spell that popped into her mind: a power spell.

Marshall, who had been waiting for the right time to jump in, now cast a dark blue water spell, to pummel Monga with the force of a waterfall. This delayed Monga's oncoming white miasma just long enough to give Mayberry time to conjure another power spell. Her spell melted into Marshall's, creating a funnel of water so fast and strong that it pierced Monga's green miasma and blasted into his body. The water swept him off his feet and sent him pinwheeling across the floor. He didn't stop until his face slammed into a stone column, hard enough for them to hear the sound of his bones breaking.

Fractures formed at the base of the column and rippled upward. It collapsed from the strain. Spinning sideways like a bowling pin, it smashed into another column, shearing it off at the base. The section of roof above the broken columns sagged; the wooden support beams moaned, then split.

Stunned, Monga stumbled out of the atrium and onto the temple's gray stone steps. He turned and faced Mayberry. His left eye had gone milky white and was bulging from its socket. He looked . . . almost . . . helpless.

"This is it!" Marshall croaked. "Let's finish him together."

"Leave, Monga. You can't defeat us now," Mayberry barked, ignoring Marshall's plea.

A strong eddy of deadly energy entered the hand brandishing the wand; she felt it urging her to kill Monga. But Mayberry had never deliberately killed any living creature. She forced her trembling hand to aim the wand's business end at the polished wood floor and waited.

Monga crouched on unsteady legs, rapidly plucking various powders from the leather pouches on his belt, which he used to weave patterns in the air in front of him. In the center of the delicate mosaic of patterns, two jawbreaker-size mint green balls appeared. With a flick of his finger, the balls broke from the mosaic and raced toward Mayberry and Marshall.

Mayberry cast a power spell to deflect the innocuous-looking green balls. Marshall's power spell melded with hers, creating a bright white force field. But Monga's balls sailed straight through the white light, like steel bullets punching through cardboard. The balls separated, raced behind Mayberry and Marshall, then punched into the center of their marks.

Mayberry felt like her body had been doused in gasoline and tossed into a bonfire. The wand spun from her burning hand as she collapsed to her knees. Beside her, she heard Marshall scream, gag, and fall to the ground. Her mind was wiped blank by the intensity of the pain. Moments later, through her tears, she glimpsed Monga's black silhouette looming over her and the metallic flash of his daggers rising to strike as she took her final breath. Death would be a welcome relief from this pain. But just before the fatal blows fell, his enormous shadow vanished.

Mayberry's pain ebbed. The wand skidded toward her on its own and bounced back into her hand. As it touched her fingers, a bath of warm energy cleared the pain away.

She vaulted to her feet and touched the mark on Marshall's

back, sharing the wand's power with him. Marshall sighed as the pain lifted, then scrambled up, ready to resume the battle.

Mayberry spotted Monga at the other end of the temple, lying on his side and desperately trying to prop himself up, using a broken stone column for support.

Without remorse, Mayberry fired off a pulse of power that drove Monga into the column with crushing force. Two other power spells joined hers, spinning him around and making it impossible for him to keep still long enough to weave another green pain spell. Monga flopped over and managed to wobble unsteadily to his feet, then groaned and stumbled toward them. Reaching deep into his warrior soul, Monga cast a magnificent orange defensive spell that deflected the power spells coming at him.

"This isn't possible!" Marshall howled.

How can he keep coming? Mayberry thought, tasting metallic terror in her mouth as she struggled to pick the spell that would take him down for good. But even as the wand helped her rapidly flip through the options, she couldn't focus long enough to select and conjure one.

Monga was almost upon them, his upper hands clenched into fists raised to strike, and his lethal daggers flashing in his lower hands.

Urrn suddenly stepped into her field of vision.

"All together this time," he said, his voice clear and calm, closing his right hand over her wand hand.

Marshall instantly followed suit, placing his left hand on top of Urrn's.

"Now!" Urrn ordered.

The wand merged three different spells into one—an unstoppable sword of vengeance. Thick streams of rainbow-colored power roared from the wand's tip, easily puncturing Monga's orange spell, then blasting into his chest with devastating ferocity.

Crack.

Monga's body shot into the air like he'd been fired from a cannon, punching a hole through the roof, then continuing to speed upward. When he finally began to plummet back to earth, his body had flown to the distant river. With a loud splash, Monga plunged into the water, then vanished under the surface for a few seconds before popping back up.

As Monga awkwardly attempted to swim back to the river-bank, a murky shadow rippled beneath him. A huge black head shot up out of the water and struck Monga like a rattle-snake. The primitive water beast's teeth slashed into Monga's left arms, then the hideous creature torqued its body over, dragging Monga down.

Just a faint trail of bubbles on the river's otherwise placid surface remained to mark Monga's last stand.

CHAPTER 42

YES!" MARSHALL SCREAMED.

The wooden supports surrounding the large hole Monga's body had made in the domed roof had started to creak and splinter. Some of the remaining stone support columns were also cracking, rivulets of dust spilling from their spreading fault lines.

"We need to get out of here," Urrn bellowed.

Mayberry glanced up at the unstable ceiling. "First I need to put this back where it belongs," she replied, holding up the wand.

Incredulous, Marshall stared at her. "Are you crazy? We need that."

"No, Marshall," Mayberry replied. "It's too powerful and too dangerous. I felt it trying to coerce me to kill Monga."

"And that was bad because . . . ?"

"Because it wasn't *me* deciding to do it," she said as she ran to the obelisk. "It needs to stay hidden."

Bits of debris were raining from the hole in the roof, scattering rubble over the temple's floor. Mayberry heard Marshall in the background, babbling about all the logical reasons she needed to keep the wand. She ignored him, pushed it back into the obelisk, and released it. For a second, she sensed that it didn't want her to let go and thought it might shoot out of the obelisk and back into her hand. But then an invisible force gripped it, turned it over, and left it hovering obediently in its rightful place.

The temple was collapsing.

Huge chunks of roof fell off like calving glaciers as more columns swayed and snapped. Mayberry sprinted for the steps, and Marshall stopped, waiting for her to catch up. When she did, he seized her hand, pulling her along so fast her feet virtually skipped across the hardwood floor.

Urrn was already hurtling across the rocks on the pond. Thankfully, none of the ammonites stirred to stop him. They were clearly designed to keep intruders *out* of the temple, not *in*.

While jumping from stone to stone, Mayberry heard loud cracks and booms as the structure collapsed behind her. When her feet touched shore, she whipped her head around just in time to watch the beautiful dome cave inward with a tremendous crash. Fragments of broken wood and stone tumbled into the pond, making waves that rocked the silent ammonites, which sank under the water and vanished.

Instead of the once magnificent temple, there was only a mountain of rubble, with a barely visible crystal lump, the top of the obelisk, poking out of the wreckage.

"You think the wand is safe there?" Marshall asked.

"I hope so," Mayberry replied.

He nudged her shoulder and smiled. "Still looked like Excalibur to me."

Mayberry smiled. "It *is* Excalibur. Or maybe the better way to say it is that everyone sees the object that—they think—makes them the most powerful."

"Weird. I still think you should have kept it. It would probably come in handy while we're hiking back to the Wishing Tree."

Sudden seeds of doubt rushed into her mind. Maybe it had been her own subconscious, not the wand, telling her to kill Monga. *Oh, well, too late now.*

CHAPTER 43

THEY RETURNED to their waiting familiars and scooped up their gear.

Co-Co jumped onto Mayberry's shoulder and nuzzled her face; Mirrt positioned himself next to Marshall, who squatted down to receive a friendly face rub followed by a lick; Uuth waddled over to assume his usual station, trailing Urrn.

"Thanks, Urrn," Marshall said earnestly. "Our plan worked. Monga forgot you were even there, and you picked the perfect time to attack to help us win the battle. Without you, we would have been toast."

"I may have waited a bit too long, let you suffer too much," Urrn said, shaking his head regretfully.

Mayberry walked over to Urrn and gave him a hug. "You may have cut it close, but our plan worked, so who cares?" she said. "I thought I was dead when Monga leaned over me with those daggers raised, then—*boom*—your power spell sent him flying."

Urrn blushed pink, and his usually somber face broke into a grin. "I know a shortcut to the aspen grove."

"Great," Mayberry exclaimed, smiling. "We can't get back fast enough."

They hit the trail with the wind at their backs and happy hearts. The temple's forlorn ruins quickly faded behind them.

As they hiked along, Urrn became chatty. "I think Monga must have been really old. Maybe even thousands of years. Think about all the centuries that different people on Earth used the power object before now—he must have somehow found out about it, then studied travelers to the Temple like Thor and Merlin until he figured out all the secrets he needed to break in."

"That makes sense," Mayberry said. "I wonder if ancients from Earth discovered the portal, then came through to build the temple. And they left it on Nith—whatever it was at the time—because they knew how dangerous it could be if it fell into the wrong hands on Earth. Then only those few who knew about the secret portal and earned the right to use it could bring it back in times of need."

"Not a bad theory," said Marshall. "A bunch of creatures from Earth's mythology were painted on the ceiling. Who knows, maybe those creatures were *real* once, and the wand or sword or whatever was used to destroy them." Marshall smiled and flexed his hands.

"Maybes on top of other bigger maybes. The truth is we have no idea who built the temple or where the original implement of power came from or what it originally looked like. Plus, when I was inside the obelisk, I saw the wand turn into objects that didn't seem to come from Earth. What do you think about all this, Urrn?" Mayberry said as she grabbed a thin tree trunk to help pull her up the next steep bit of the ridge they were hiking on.

Urrn reached a hand down to help her keep her balance, then changed the subject. "Well, you came through the portal by accident, not to do penance like me. That's why I decided that it wouldn't be right to let Monga keep you."

"Whatever you did wrong on Earth must have happened decades ago," Mayberry replied in a choppy cadence as she struggled to keep her balance on the sharp ridge. "Don't you think you've atoned by now? Plus, you've saved two lives— mine and Marshall's."

"What did you do that makes you think you deserve punishment?" Marshall asked, completely baffled.

Annoyed by the question, Urrn suddenly frowned, fell silent, and continued tramping. For a while they walked silently too, but they couldn't stay quiet for long, and were soon reliving and dissecting their harrowing experiences.

At the end of the day, they used Monga's supplies to pitch camp. Guarded by their familiars, they all slept like babies that night.

The next morning, Marshall opened his eyes when Mirrt's

tongue licked his face. He gave his pet a hug and looked around. Although the jungle hadn't changed much, the air smelled different today. He had a good feeling. He roused the others and soon they were all back on the trail.

After a few hours, they topped a bushy rise. Urrn pointed at the valley below. "That's what we're looking for."

Marshall tented a hand over his eyes and looked out. Sure enough, there was the aspen grove in the distance, its leaves a blur of shimmering gold.

"That's it," Mayberry cried in delight. "That's our grove."

He could see by her open face and broad smile that she hadn't been this happy in . . . well, he couldn't remember when. Mayberry enthusiastically grabbed Marshall and Urrn and hugged them, patted Uuth, squeezed Co-Co, and let Mirrt lick her face. Then she grabbed Marshall's hand, and he jogged down the hill with her, overflowing with excitement.

"Urrn," Marshall hollered, seeing him hanging back, "we're almost there. You're *free*. It's time for you to come home."

"I'm going to stay," Urrn said. He pointed to a large dark hole at the corner of the big rocky hill in the distance. "There. That was my home before I met the Sleviccs. And before Monga captured me."

Marshall and Mayberry started walking back uphill toward Urrn. "You're going to stay here and live in a *cave*?"

It was hard for them to understand, but Urrn seemed relieved to have found the cave. "Yes."

Marshall took a few steps closer and held out a hand. "If

you come back to Earth with us, you'll have a house to live in. Remember? Your parents, cookies, snow, all that stuff?"

"Nith is my home now," Urrn said, shaking his head at Marshall's outstretched hand. "My parents might not even be alive. And even if they were, they wouldn't want me anymore. The Sleviccs are my friends—I can find them again. And I can't go back until I *know* that my punishment is over."

Mayberry and Marshall looked at each other, and Mayberry shook her head. The reality was that they knew very little about Urrn's previous life. Maybe he'd committed a serious crime on Earth, and going back would mean trading one kind of prison for another.

"Go," Urrn said, smiling weakly and waving them on. "It's time for you to go home." He turned toward the cave and began to walk away, with Uuth shuffling faithfully along behind him.

"We made it back to the portal, Mayberry," Marshall declared with a rush of unfettered joy.

He threw his arms open to invite her in. She wrapped her arms snugly around him. As she tilted her head back to look into his eyes, he couldn't help himself; he pressed his lips against hers.

Mayberry's lips tasted like strawberries. Marshall felt his head spin and cheeks tingle when he felt her kissing him back. A current of pleasure rushed from his head to his toes. Was this love? He didn't know, but what he did know was that he had never felt happier.

He took a moment to hug Mirrt and bid him farewell, as did Mayberry with Co-Co. The comfortable buzz in his head told him that Mirrt understood why Marshall had to leave. Purring, Co-Co climbed onto Mirrt's back, then scampered onto his right head, gripping his ear with her front paws. Mirrt rested serenely on his haunches, watching as the duo turned away and walked across the grassy meadow to the aspen forest.

Marshall removed the stick he'd been using to keep track of time from his backpack. He counted them silently, then said, "Sixteen cuts, so we've been here a little more than sixteen days. Seems like longer, doesn't it?" he said, handing it to Mayberry.

"It sure does," she replied, breaking the stick in half and tossing it away. "We won't be needing that anymore."

The GPS in Marshall's gut navigated them straight back to the Tree.

And there it was, just as shining, beautiful, and imposing as before. It was a world unto itself, a unique ecosystem of life and leaves and branches. They collapsed together into a happy bundle under the Tree. They didn't have to practice their wish, since they'd talked about it so often.

"I hope this works. We don't have a backup plan." Mayberry sounded a bit concerned.

"Wishing Tree, please take us back to the same place where we left Earth. Now. Together," Marshall and Mayberry said.

As his eyes slowly closed, Marshall thought, *Nith healed our spirits. Being here is the hardest thing we've ever done, but neither of us will ever be the same again.*

He glimpsed leaves beginning to whirl around them, and then he fell sound asleep and couldn't see or hear anything at all.

The Tree granted their wish.

CHAPTER 44

MAYBERRY FELT like she'd just closed her eyes, but now was a bit groggy. She remembered lying down by the Wishing Tree and wishing, and that vivid, bizarre images had started floating in her mind. She became conscious of the warm arm wrapped around her waist, and then the arm withdrew, leaving her feeling slightly chilled.

She blinked her eyes open to inky darkness. Why had she slept for so long? Leaves rustled in the breeze, and birds trilled in the distance. She saw Marshall getting to his feet, adjusting his glasses on his nose. Her mind wrestled with an emotional conundrum she couldn't begin to explain. She'd felt so comfortable in his arms. What had happened? In her dream, Marshall had lost his glasses, but now he was wearing them. Marshall reached down and took Mayberry's hand, pulling her to her feet.

"I guess we fell asleep. No other world with magic, after all. I had some weird dreams, though," Mayberry said quietly in a sleepy voice.

"Okay," he responded curtly, his shoulders drooping a bit. Maybe waking up with his arms wrapped around her had mortified him. Without meeting her eyes, he used his pocketknife to saw a long branch from the giant tree.

Marshall clicked the button on his flashlight, but it didn't work. He shook his head and gingerly handed Mayberry the branch he'd cut for her to use as a walking stick. She felt a strange tingle as her hand touched the branch.

"Marshall, I had an amazing dream. I want to tell you—"

"Can we please talk about your dreams another time?" Marshall said, interrupting her. "We're actually lost in the woods—the woods where people who get lost are never found again?"

Even though Mayberry agreed that bumbling around the woods at night wasn't the best idea, she wasn't sure why Marshall was taking their situation so personally. His attitude was especially annoying, because her last clear memory was . . . well . . . of kissing him. She remembered that the kissing part was *good*, but the dream hadn't been *all* good—there'd also been flashes of fighting, and running from something that wanted to hurt them, and good and bad magic.

She pushed up the sleeves of her jacket and examined her arms for bruises or scrapes. But her skin was unblemished. Bits of leaves and debris from sleeping on the ground clung

Was this love?

to her clothing, but . . . *Nothing happened. Nothing changed. Nothing at all. But why do I feel so strongly that it had?*

Marshall occasionally glanced her way while they hiked out of the forest. It was dark, but it seemed like Marshall was mad, or maybe sad. Mayberry didn't think she'd done anything to make him angry, but it didn't seem like the right time to ask.

After almost an hour, they exited the forest, crossed the bridge and meadow, and reached the bushes where they'd stashed their bikes. Mayberry whipped out her cell phone, which was finally working. It was nearly three thirty in the morning, and it was *Sunday.* Over eighteen hours had passed since they'd left home Saturday morning, and they'd slept for sixteen of them. How was that even possible? Mayberry responded to her parents' frantic late-night texts asking where she was and told them she'd been having phone trouble but everything was okay and she would call them in the morning.

Marshall silently handed her the aspen samples he'd cut while hiking to the big tree, and she crammed them into her pockets. After strapping the walking stick onto her bike as a souvenir, they mounted up and began to pedal home together.

When they reached the junction, Marshall peeled his bike toward his house, waving a hand in her direction but not even saying good-bye. It had started as a good day—Mayberry wasn't sure where it had gone wrong. At the very least they could claim a victory: they'd made it to the middle of the Mystery Forest, and even though it hadn't worked, they'd actually *found* the Wishing Tree.

CHAPTER 45

MAYBERRY BRUSHED HER TEETH, scrunched into her plaid flannel PJs, and flopped into bed, feeling way more tired than she should, given the marathon nap she'd just taken.

She fell asleep, then woke up in a cold sweat a few hours later. She'd been dreaming about the strangest creatures—a four-armed green troll, Bigfoots, and a river monster with deadly tentacles and a huge maw. *Must be anxiety dreams.* She rolled out of bed and wandered restlessly around the house, looking through piles of magazines and watching bad late-night TV. Before long, she headed back to bed, pushed her head into the soft pillow, and after some fitful tossing and turning, trying to quell the strange images floating up from her subconscious, drifted off again.

She woke up around noon with her fingers squeezing her

blanket so tightly she nearly had to pry them off. More incredibly vivid dreams had swum to the surface of her muddled brain.

She tossed the covers aside and jumped out of bed. She was hungry—famished, actually. When she'd gotten back she'd been way too tired to put something together for herself. She hadn't eaten since the snacks Marshall had given her on their way into the aspen grove. Thank God her mother wasn't home. She would have served Mayberry fresh fruit and mint tea instead of the bacon and egg fiesta that she craved. She slogged into the kitchen and went to work, then ate the results like eating was her job. She topped off the meal by gulping down a few mugs of black coffee to juice her brain.

She needed something to distract her from the crazy dreams and her now-tenuous relationship with Marshall, so she carried the tree samples Marshall had taken from the grove—along with another full mug of coffee—up to her mom's lab. Then she remembered the walking stick strapped to her bike, and went back downstairs to collect that, too.

With a sharp blade, Mayberry cut slices from all the perimeter trees' branches, then fired up the electron microscope. This microscope would scan each slice and transfer all the data it gathered, including DNA, into her mom's computer. Another program would analyze the DNA from the individual slices while simultaneously comparing that data with every other sample that had been inputted. This resulted in an overlapping graphic that displayed all the chosen samples' similarities and differences.

Mayberry began inputting the slices and running the programs. The repetitive work was soothing, and soon she'd forgotten all about her dreams. Now she was just another lab drone, inputting data and waiting patiently for the results to be calculated. She was taking another sip of coffee from her mug when she looked up and saw the results displayed on the computer monitor. Her hand trembled, and she sloshed coffee on her lab coat.

The samples taken by Marshall from various points around the grove—even the trees farthest away from each other—were *exact matches*, which meant that all the samples came from the same aspen tree. She may have found a quaking aspen colony!

Another piece of the puzzle was her hiking stick. If a sample taken from the Wishing Tree in the center of the grove matched, perhaps after taking more samples around the perimeter of the whole aspen grove she could confirm that the whole grove was actually one gigantic organism. This could change her mother's life—and *her* life—forever.

She cut a slice from from the walking stick and tested it.

Uh-oh. So maybe her life hadn't changed after all, except for being the proud owner of a coffee-stained lab coat. The Wishing Tree's sample didn't match the perimeter samples at all, which meant that only *part* of the grove was one interlaced tree, and so she had no idea how big it really was without further research.

She inputted the data from the samples into her mom's

database to compare them with DNA from other quaking aspens. Her eyebrows arched with astonishment.

Very strange. The DNA templates from the perimeter trees didn't match those of any similar quaking aspen species. Mayberry's brain snapped to attention. She expanded her search from quaking aspens to the DNA templates common to all trees. None of them even approximated a match, which *theoretically* indicated that this grove was a totally unique organism.

Maybe the data had been corrupted—the samples could have been contaminated in Marshall's pack. Mayberry widened the search, but only turned up DNA markers that were common to all carbon-based life forms. The grove's DNA apparently had as much in common with humans, birds, and other animals as it did with trees. It made no sense.

There was one more set of tests to run. She used her mom's sterile core borer on the walking stick this time, to be sure she got a clean sample, then mounted and scanned it. She labeled the walking stick MF CENTER 1, then walked over to her bedroom and tossed it in the closet so it wouldn't get mixed up with the other samples.

When she got back to the office, she examined the conclusion. The results from her prior test samples had been shocking, but this one was even more outlandish. The DNA strands from the stick didn't have an identifiable relationship to any other organism on Earth.

She reran all the tests, using every instrument at her disposal, and kept getting the same results. A low-grade headache began to crawl between her eyes.

Reluctantly, she took a break, going into the kitchen to fix a "mom meal": an organic salad with all the trimmings. As she chewed, she reviewed what she knew. The only organisms on Earth that were so distinctive they weren't directly related to anything else in nature and sometimes not even to each other were one of the most diverse groups on Earth: simple slime molds. Slime molds typically existed as single-celled individuals. However, under certain conditions, one cell could combine with another, becoming a mobile slug and actually altering its DNA in the process—changing from a plant to an animal. Geneticists believed that a species being able to alter its own DNA was impossible, but in the case of slime molds, it wasn't.

The DNA from the aspens in the grove was infinitely more complex than that of slime molds, and yet wasn't even close to matching any other organism in her mom's database. But the fact was, she was just a high school kid trained to slog through routine samplings. She wasn't supposed to be using her mom's cutting-edge lab equipment on her own—for entertainment or her own scientific investigation. Mayberry decided not to tell her mom about her trip into the Mystery Forest or about any of the bizarre test results until she came up with a rational explanation, but how could she solve this scientific dilemma by herself?

CHAPTER 46

THE REST OF Mayberry's Sunday activities were in-consequential. If she'd been home in New York, she would have been hanging out with her friends, but here, without Marshall, all she had to do was watch TV or listen to music. She missed him.

Even though things had been inexplicably weird the last time they saw each other, she decided to call him anyway.

"Finally," she said when he picked up. "It feels like I've been waiting to talk to you for days."

There was a pause, and then she heard the sound of Marshall tapping his fingers on something. "Yeah," he grumbled. "I've just been here working on some freelance stuff. What are you doing?"

"Nothing much," Mayberry said. "Well, some stuff in my

mom's lab, but we can talk about that later. You know . . . I still want to tell you about that dream I had. It was so strange."

"Mayberry, I really don't want to talk about the dreams we had while we were passed out in the woods," he said abruptly. "That giant tree stoked our imaginations. I had a weird dream too, but I think we should just let it go."

Mayberry sighed. She knew her dream couldn't be real, but why wouldn't he talk about it?

"Okay, then," Marshall said. "See you tomorrow."

He hung up.

Mayberry lowered her cell phone, shaking her head in dismay. She couldn't stop thinking about her dreams, her lab test results were crazy, and on top of everything, Marshall was growing distant just when she felt like they should be closer than ever. She knew that in real life he wasn't the heroic savior he'd been in her fantasy dream, even if her heart kept insisting otherwise.

Mayberry drifted to the TV console and pawed through her father's old DVD collection until found one she hadn't seen before—a goofy seventies movie called *Animal House*. Hopefully watching a vintage frat-boy comedy would take her mind off of how weird everything was feeling.

The sound of Mayberry's sweet voice had bitten into Marshall like an iron claw squeezing his heart. His eyeballs felt like they were drooping out of his head, and he had a fierce headache no pill could relieve. He had to stop talking to her before he confessed something he couldn't take back—like how he couldn't stop thinking about her—or blurted out how he imagined them being really . . . a couple in love.

Marshall's parents hadn't noticed he'd been out last night way after midnight, and now he was fixing himself a box of macaroni and cheese in the kitchen while they sat in their chairs. He'd been having some pretty vivid dreams, too, and they felt even more real than their bike ride to the forest. In his dream, he'd been brave, and tough, and resourceful, and so was Mayberry. Together, they'd been unstoppable.

But back in the real world, life was exactly the same. He was the same dork he'd always been. Still, there was one thing really messing with his head: after his morning shower, he'd noticed a swirling red mark between his shoulder blades— exactly like the one that monster named Monga had put on him in his dream. Logic told him his back was probably inflamed because he'd been eaten alive by bugs while sleeping under the tree, which would explain why he had dreamed about the mark. He was good with that.

Now if only he could think of a way to put his shattered spirit back together . . .

CHAPTER 47

ON MONDAY MORNING, the high school's scuffed black-and-white-checked floors, smudged yellow walls, and cork bulletin boards made Marshall uneasy. He preferred to imagine himself holding hands with Mayberry as they walked through fragrant forests and grassy fields.

His mind didn't accept being back on Earth at school until right after lunch in chemistry class, when a switch in his head flipped on and his brain landed in his body so that both were finally occupying the same space. The chemistry teacher was helping a few students near the rear wall, with his back to the rest of the class. Marshall fidgeted by a metal work counter, trying to concentrate on his experiment. It was hard because Jim was amusing his comrades by tossing a cork-topped test tube full of acid from hand to hand.

Exasperated, Marshall put his test tube in its rack and stepped around the counter. "You need to stop doing that."

"Are you kidding?" Jim said with a smirk and another toss of the test tube. "Why are you even talking to me, creep?"

"I'm *talking* to you because you're going to hurt someone with that acid," Marshall replied, his nostrils flaring, nodding his head to indicate India Hankie, who was working at the bench behind Jim.

Jim's jaw tightened. "Did you hear that? Jackson's trying to tell me what to do." He glanced over his shoulder to confirm that the teacher was still busy. "Are you going to *make* me stop, Jackson?"

Marshall paused and stared into Jim's dull eyes for a moment. Jim had made his life miserable for as long as he could remember. He'd been pushed, punched, and generally humiliated. But this encounter felt different. He just . . . wasn't intimidated anymore. Jim wasn't even as scary as an average housecat.

Marshall raised his eyebrows. "If you don't decide to stop right now, I *will* make you stop."

Jim's face flushed pink. "Is this a new you, Jackson?" he said, waggling the test tube near Marshall's face. "I can't wait to see you make me."

Then he tossed the test tube into the air with his right hand, intending to catch it behind his back with his left—but it flew off course. It was about to shatter on India's table when, lightning fast, Marshall vaulted over the counter and snatched it out of the air.

Oblivious to her narrow escape, India looked up from her worksheet and saw Marshall holding a test tube above her head.

"What are you doing?" she asked, bewildered.

"Nothing," he replied, pushing the test tube firmly into the holder on Jim's table. "Jim, do us all a favor and try not to touch that again. You're not smart enough to play with chemicals."

The students around them snickered, and a few even broke into spontaneous applause. His teacher, oblivious to the unfolding adolescent drama, lifted his head to see what was happening, then noticed the time.

"Class dismissed," he called out as the bell rang. "Put your projects in your cubbies. We'll finish up on Wednesday."

Jim stared at Marshall, gaping in disbelief as the rest of the class began to shuffle their papers and projects. The inexplicable confrontation and demonstration of Marshall's athleticism made him feel like like a bat had been applied to the back of his head.

Marshall smirked, then bolted out the door, heading for his locker.

CHAPTER 48

THAT WAS . . . THAT WAS . . . *awesome*, Marshall thought a few minutes later, as he strolled across the gym's wooden basketball court. He heard the sounds of dribbling, followed by the faint *whoosh* of something speeding toward him, so he instinctively spun around. Three basketballs were on a collision course with his head. He shifted slightly to the right, and the first one ripped by his left ear. He stopped the second one with his right hand and grabbed the third with his left.

Jim and his two closest friends were standing in a neat row, throwing arms still extended. Marshall smirked and decided on the spot to name the three amigos the Wit brothers—Jim was Dim, and the others were Nit and Half.

With a smooth, powerful lateral movement of his right arm, he whipped a basketball back at the surprised gang. It smacked into the gym floor a couple feet in front of Nit, then ricocheted into his solar plexus, bowling him over. The basketball rebounded into Half's chin, clipping his head back so sharply that he tumbled roughly to the ground.

Two down, Dim to go, Marshall thought, grinning.

His face reflecting the first hint of fear, Jim bent his knees into a basketball player's defensive crouch, with his hands pushed out to grab or deflect the remaining ball.

Showing off, Marshall spun the basketball on his right index finger, then let it slide into his palm. He rocketed it up so high that it disappeared into the shadows cast by the gym's rafters. It bounced off the ceiling and rushed down, smacking Jim squarely on the forehead. He collapsed onto the floor, goggle-eyed, sucking for breath like a goldfish tossed out of water.

Zen calm, Marshall patiently crossed his arms over his chest, waiting to see what would happen next.

Jim scrambled awkwardly to his feet. His forehead sported an ugly red welt, and his face had contorted into a mask of fury. He charged toward Marshall with his right fist cocked back and up, screaming and cursing.

It seemed to Marshall that the dimwitted fool's body was moving toward him in slow motion. When Jim was just a foot away, Marshall agilely sidestepped so Jim's fist breezed by its intended target: his face. Then Marshall swift-kicked Jim in the rear as he flew past. The perfectly timed blow knocked Jim off his feet, and he landed hard on his back. Dazed, he popped up off the floor faster than common sense dictated and stumbled awkwardly toward Marshall, struggling to keep his fists up.

Marshall went on the offensive. He rushed forward, grabbed Jim's right wrist, and before his opponent could react, used it as a lever to jerk him forward while driving his left elbow into Jim's exposed sternum. Jim howled in agony and fell to his knees.

The other two Wit brothers had regained their footing, but stood back out of harm's way, watching with mute horror as their friend was being methodically whipped. They were too afraid—or too smart—to jump in and help.

Any opponent with half a brain would have thrown in the towel and begged for mercy. But Jim was different. Like a zombie on steroids, he lurched to his feet again, readying himself for one final, desperate gambit: a blind, wobbly, head-down bull rush. Because Jim was, well, really Dim, Marshall decided it would be easy to play the same trick again, so he waited for him to get close enough, then dodged aside. Before Jim's body skidded past his, Marshall landed a lightning-quick left-right combo to his ribs. Jim buckled over, then vomited up his lunch on the gym's shiny floor.

Marshall looked up and beckoned to the two stunned rubbernecking Wit brothers, who both fled the scene like ducks at the first blast of a shotgun.

"I guess we're done here, Jim," Marshall said with a smile. "I hope you don't have to 'make me' tell you what to do again."

CHAPTER 49

S TUDENTS WEREN'T ALLOWED to keep their phones on while they were in the school building, but Mayberry had never been good at following rules. Her history teacher, Ms. Kendall, was just discussing a World War I battle when Mayberry's phone vibrated. She slipped it out of her pocket and glanced down.

It was from Marshall: **Com2 nurse's offc, 911.**

In class, she texted back.

911!!!!

Mayberry tucked her phone away and raised her hand. Ms. Kendall used her pointer to acknowledge Mayberry.

"May I please be excused? I need to go to the nurse's office."

Ms. Kendall's lips turned down. "There are only fifteen minutes of class remaining, Mayberry. Do you think you can—"

"I think I might be sick, Ms. Kendall," she said. "I mean . . . vomit."

Ms. Kendall wrinkled her nose and waved her out with the pointer. "Feel better, dear."

Mayberry gathered her books and boogied down to the nurse's office. As usual, the nurse wasn't there, because there was only one nurse to serve two school districts. Mayberry wasn't happy about rushing to see Marshall the second he beckoned, especially considering how he'd been acting. As she entered the nurse's office, she saw Marshall sitting on the edge of the examining table, swinging his legs back and forth, looking loveable and cute. In spite of herself, she smiled a little.

"Okay, I'm here," she said frostily. "What's the emergency?"

Marshall jumped off the table and walked over to Mayberry, looking down at her with his warm brown eyes. "First of all, I want to apologize. I've been rude, or avoiding you, and I'm really sorry."

Mayberry rolled her eyes a little. This was a good start. "Okay. Apology accepted."

Marshall leaned back against the table. "I need to tell you what just happened. Jim was tossing a test tube of acid around and would have shattered it on this girl's desk and smoked her, but I went all superhero and snatched it out of midair."

"That's . . . unusual."

"After class, Jim and his friends tried to jump me, but I kicked his ass and scared the hell out of his buddies."

Mayberry's eyes widened. "You're saying that you snatched acid out of the air, then beat up Jim. Maybe you've turned into an X-Man or something."

"Show me your back," Marshall said, twirling a finger around.

"Excuse me?" Mayberry said.

"Just humor me and let me look at your back for a second?"

"Okay, okay," she said. She turned and allowed him to stretch down the fabric of her sweater to expose her upper back.

A shiver coursed through Mayberry's body as Marshall touched her between the shoulder blades.

"It's there," he said softly.

"What's there?"

"Monga's mark."

"No way," she said, thinking, *How does he know about Monga?*

"Look in the mirror."

Confounded, she maneuvered until she could see her back in the mirror. In the middle, three inches above her bra strap, was a red swirl.

"I have one that looks exactly the same," he said, turning around and lifting his own shirt to show her. "I think we actually went to Nith."

Mayberry's mind blazed as she recollected flashes of all the "dreams" she'd been struggling to forget. The Sleviccs, Monga, Co-Co. It was if she and Marshall had lived and forgotten a whole lifetime together.

He pulled his sweater down and turned around. "You didn't say *Who's Monga?* or *What's Nith?*"

Even though Mayberry had been confused by the bizarre images and her feelings for Marshall before, now she was really struggling to keep herself together. Magic wasn't real. Science was real. She groped for a sensible response, but finding one was like trying to hold on to water shooting from a fire hose.

"Things you believe can manifest physically," she countered. "Lots of people have psychosomatic illnesses—they *think* they're sick, so they exhibit real symptoms."

"Okay, but how did we *both* dream the exact *same* dream and *both* create the same marks on our backs?"

"I can't explain that," Mayberry said, shaking her head. "But, as far as Jim goes, maybe it's just that you finally got pissed enough to do what you could have done all along. Look, Marshall, we both know Nith couldn't have happened. We thought we were there for over two weeks, but we were only asleep for sixteen hours."

Marshall leaned back on the examining table and closed his eyes, thinking. "Maybe the tree exuded a pheromone that made us hallucinate together or something? My memories are so clear . . . and they seem so *real.*"

"Mine do too," Mayberry said, taking his hands in hers and squeezing. "We're a little crazy, aren't we?"

"I don't think so," he said, pulling her in close. "I think we're the sanest people around."

Mayberry tilted her face up, bringing her lips tantalizingly close to his. He leaned down, and kissed her, just as he had in the dream. She clearly remembered the feel and taste of his lips, and their intimacy seemed perfectly natural and right. This was all . . . to say the least . . . very surprising. But the how and the why still eluded her bewildered brain.

CHAPTER 50

WORD OF JIM'S astonishing debacle spread through the school like wildfire. No one was unhappy that the bully had been exposed as a mere mortal, but they were shocked to hear who had delivered the ass-kicking. The next day, many of the boys nodded respectfully when they crossed Marshall's path, and more than one of the girls looked him over.

After scrutinizing him with fresh eyes, they decided that he was much cuter than they'd recalled, and a few found reasons to talk to him. Girls had never before given him even a whiff of attention, and he had no idea how to behave, so he smiled and made awkward chitchat, but otherwise tried to ignore them.

After their final class, Mayberry and Marshall met and strolled hand in hand over to her house. Yesterday, after they'd kissed, and then kissed some more, she'd brought him up to date on her strange test results and wanted to show him what she'd found.

Since Mayberry's mom and dad were still away, when Marshall came over, he settled comfortably into her mom's desk chair. He leaned in and booted up one of the computers while Mayberry sat in front of a worktable and did the same.

"I've been thinking about the DNA problem you described, and I did a few hours of research for you last night," Marshall said. "Scientists studying ancient bone fossils use CT scanners to find organic molecules. Then they use DNA mapping to investigate them at the molecular level. They can find DNA fragments that are hundreds of millions of years old—pollen, spores . . . things like that. They even extracted DNA from a mummified hadrosaur."

"I've read about that *Jurassic World* stuff," Mayberry said, warming to the idea that he had worked so hard last night to help her.

"The School of Environmental Sciences in England has the leading experts on this," Marshall said, rolling the chair back and forth while he spoke. "Last night I sort of . . . hacked my way into their data banks and poked around."

"You did *what*?"

"I have no idea how to decode it all, but I can pull it up right now," he said. "It could help."

Ping.

The data came through seconds later, and Mayberry opened the first PDF, which exhibited an artist's rendering of a prehistoric tree. She closed it and opened another image: an apatosaurus browsing on the foliage at the top of a towering palm. All the images had DNA samples attached in a separate data packet.

Mayberry recalibrated her mom's equipment to compare the DNA from the ancient fragments to the DNA samples she'd taken from the aspen trees and walking stick. Once she did, she determined that there were numerous differences, especially with the walking stick's DNA sample, which didn't match anything they had. But at least with the other samples, there were similarities, too—more than she'd found with anything that lived on Earth *now*. Could the samples from the aspen grove's trees that were attached to the main root ball organism really be *that* old? Hundreds of millions of years old? Older? That's what this data implied. She showed Marshall the results.

"That's amazing," he said.

"Yeah," Mayberry said. "Amazing in the purest sense of the word. Meaning completely implausible. I'm not doing the analysis wrong; it's just that the results make zero sense, especially for the big tree in the center, whose DNA doesn't correlate to any other species, including the other aspens in the grove."

"Yeah. Well, there's a lot about DNA we don't understand, right? More than ninety-seven percent of human DNA is the same as the DNA in apes. It's the three percent that makes humans unique."

"Sure does, Marshall. So what we have here, folks," she proclaimed, her cadence and voice mimicking that of a carnival barker, "is a giant tree that is hundreds of millions of years old. And guess what else? It looks exactly like an ordinary aspen, but it isn't one . . . so it must be wearing a clever disguise."

CHAPTER 51

THEY STARED AT EACH OTHER for a second and then Marshall said, "Let's get back online and see what else we can find out about the Mystery Forest."

"On it," Mayberry replied.

She started digging. There were rumors and tall tales aplenty, but it was hard to figure out if any of the stories were grounded in reality. There was an article about a hiker who got lost inside the forest for weeks before he was finally found passed out on its edge, dehydrated, hypothermic, and starving, having walked holes in the soles of his shoes. That one might have been true. The story of a saucer-shaped spaceship hovering above the aspen grove and using a magnetic ray to suck up all the deer, rabbits, and birds in a one-mile radius was likely false. Both stories were hearsay.

"Wow," Marshall said, perplexed. He rolled the chair over to look at the computer screen.

He'd found an article on the front page of the *Eden Grove Gazette* from about a year and a half ago. The headline was MISSING BOY FOUND. A big color photo in the middle of the page showed the headshot of a sharp-featured boy with an unruly shock of red hair, who had a smudge or maybe a birthmark on his right cheek. The photo's caption read *Aaron Fitzsimmons Rescued*.

Marshall summed up the contents of the newspaper article for her: "Aaron and his younger sister, Laura, were playing in Thomas Park, and Laura ran out onto the ice that covered the pond. The ice cracked, and she fell through. Aaron did everything he could, but she drowned."

"That's sad," Mayberry replied.

"Yeah, but wait until you hear the rest. Aaron was really upset, and he left home to take a bike ride the day of Laura's funeral. But he didn't come back, and after twenty-four hours they formed a search party. A forest ranger found a kid's tracks in the meadow by the Mystery Forest and followed them for miles, and finally found him deep in the Mystery Forest. Aaron was breathing, but he was in a coma. The ranger carried him out."

"The forest ranger who rescued him couldn't have been the guy we saw," Mayberry said with a chuckle. "That dude couldn't lug a grapefruit out of the forest."

Marshall leaned into the computer and touched the photo on the screen. "Look at him, Mayberry. Wouldn't you say that Aaron looks a lot like Urrn? A younger version of him, obviously, but still . . . I thought Urrn looked familiar when we first met him, but I couldn't quite place him. Aaron was a year behind me at school. And Aaron sounds sort of like *Urrn*, doesn't it?"

Mayberry's skin began to crawl. It was impossible, but everything that had happened was impossible. "See if he's still in a coma."

While Marshall's fingers began flying over the keyboard, Mayberry decided to take a cookie-baking break. For once she was happy to be doing it, not trying to bury a bad day.

CHAPTER 52

HALF AN HOUR LATER, Marshall snatched a fresh cookie from the plate Mayberry offered, gulped it down, and grabbed another. He smiled. "I'll make the next batch of cookies—promise."

"Sure," said Mayberry.

Marshall pushed back from the desk. "So . . . Aaron is alive and still in a coma. A blogger who works at Methodist United says his parents visit him all the time. It's weird—he's brain-dead, but his body kept growing normally and his muscles didn't wither away—which never happens."

"Wait a minute," Mayberry said her brain kicking into overdrive. "We know our bodies didn't come with us when we went to Nith, because when we got back, our clothes were clean and you were wearing the glasses you'd lost on Nith. We did bring back those marks Monga made on us—but he used magic for that. Hypothetically, suppose the Wishing Tree took our minds to a world in another dimension, where they inhabited shadow bodies or clones or something. Our Earth bodies stayed under the tree, and it would seem to people here like we were in comas and brain-dead, too, until our minds woke up back in our Earth bodies."

Marshall nodded. "Well, if we're going all in, then, we should also look at a possible time shift between dimensions. It's about a full day on Nith for every Earth hour, which explains our weird perception of the time differences between the worlds. That also explains why Aaron's body is fourteen years old here, but middle-aged on Nith."

Rapidly gathering her thoughts, Mayberry said, "Last year I read a book called *Endless Universe*. The authors think that there are probably multiple universes and that parts of them intersect at times. Maybe if someone asks it the right way, the Tree is able to teleport their minds into an alternative intersecting universe."

"Weird," Marshall said, tapping his fingers on the desk. He whirled back to the keyboard. "What the hell. Let's look at Aaron."

"How are we going to do that? Are you going to hack into the hospital's security cameras or something?"

Marshall responded with a waterfall of clacking keys, "Yup. They don't protect access to the cams the way they do patient records."

In a few minutes, a boy's outline flashed live on their monitor. A nurse was carefully sponging off Aaron's inert body.

Mayberry leaned in and stared at the image. She thought she recognized the sleeping face, but he was so much younger, it was hard to be sure. Then the nurse flipped him onto his side to wash his back and untied his green hospital gown. She opened it up, revealing Monga's mark, a red, raised spiral between his shoulder blades.

"Oh my God," Mayberry breathed. "It's Urrn, all right. Now what are we going to do?"

"I don't know, but we'd better do it fast," Marshall responded, zooming in the security camera's lens to focus on the medical chart attached to the foot of the bed.

On it, bold red type declared *Termination Procedure Authorized at 7:00 P.M.*

"That's it, then," Marshall blurted out in dismay. "We have to go back to Nith, right now, and find Aaron or he'll *die*—on Earth and in Nith."

Mayberry looked at Marshall, her eyes scrunched. "I agree we have to go. He saved us. But that doesn't mean I'm not scared."

Marshall slid his chair back. "I'll get my gear and meet you back here in half an hour."

"Let's do it," Mayberry said. "I'll pack food and water."

Mayberry had started walking down the stairs with Marshall when an epiphany struck. When her feet touched the ground floor, she whirled and began to concentrate. Gray power pulsed around her fingers. She aimed them at a heavy book resting on an end table. The faint gray glow shot from her fingers, lifting the book off the table and sending it flying against the wall.

Nith had happened, and everything modern science believed about the nature of the universe was totally wrong.

"Sick," Marshall said, taken aback. "I figured Nith was a dream, so I never even *tried* to do magic here."

"Me neither—and that was really hard. Our magic is weaker here. Or maybe it's just fading."

CHAPTER 53

WHEN MARSHALL GOT TO HIS HOUSE, he ignored his parents and scurried upstairs. Grabbing his backpack, he threw in his Swiss army knife, a Leatherman tool, some rope, a poncho, a couple of water bottles, and various snacks. Then he went to the medicine cabinet and plucked out a tube of antiseptic ointment and a small box of bandages before rushing down the stairs.

He was already heading out the front door when he remembered something else that might prove useful. A couple of years earlier, his dad had purchased a "home protection" weapon he couldn't afford, mostly because he thought it looked cool. It was a western-style Uberti revolver with an extra-long barrel, pearl grip, and scroll engraving. Marshall rushed upstairs into his parents' room and opened up the drawer in his dad's nightstand. There it was, resting in its leather holster, along with a box of .45-caliber ammunition. He loaded it and stuffed it in his backpack—just in case. *Yee-ha.* He felt powerful—invincible even—and suddenly understood why carrying handguns could be so dangerous, even if he wasn't sure if this type of Earth technology would work on Nith. He didn't expect to need the gun, but he was ready for action either way.

Marshall jumped on his bike and rode to Mayberry's house. She was already waiting for him outside.

They coasted into the Mystery Forest parking lot and stuffed their bikes into the same shrubs they'd used before. Approaching the split-rail fence, they kept their eyes focused on the slat bench next to the ranger's cabin. They figured that he'd be around at this time of day, so they'd just make a dash for the fence, scramble over it, and sprint into the forest before he could stop them.

There was no need.

The ranger was lying flat on the bench. He knuckled his sleepy eyes, yawned, and rolled over with his back to them. It was easy to slip past him and head for the forest.

Crossing into the aspen grove felt different this time. The fading, gold-tinged light was welcoming, like an old friend with open arms. They both knew exactly how to find the Tree. It was like a beacon drawing them close. When they arrived, they were once again amazed by its massive scale and indescribable beauty. The vibe from the Tree when they touched its base was warm and comfortable.

"I guess we should lie down," Mayberry said. "Are you . . . er . . . feeling sleepy?"

"Ha-ha," Marshall said. "Not really. But I guess the Tree will take care of that part." His hands slid along the pale bark as he lowered himself to the leaf-strewn ground.

Mayberry lay down beside Marshall and entwined her fingers with his, then used her other hand to reach out and make contact with the bark.

Marshall closed his eyes, and images from Nith swam in his head. The swift rushing river, the thick forests that teemed with bizarre wildlife, the sheer joy of running faster than humanly possible . . . all this merged, then blurred.

"We wish to go back to Nith together," Marshall said, yawning.

Mayberry sleepily confirmed, "I agree."

A moment passed, then golden leaves blew in a circle around them as the Tree granted their wish.

CHAPTER 54

E RIC FITZSIMMONS GRIPPED the thin metal arms of the visitor's chair. His wife, Carol, rested one hand on his right shoulder and pressed a tissue to her nose with the other. A prim, white-clad nurse scurried around the small room with brisk efficiency, checking Aaron's vital signs for the last time. Carol didn't see the point. The medical staff was preparing to disconnect her son's life support. He'd be dead just a few minutes later.

"Mrs. Fitzsimmons. Mr. Fitzsimmons."

Dr. Buddingham approached, holding his clipboard. He was the doctor who'd finally convinced them that Aaron's mind was already gone and never coming back.

"It's time to go."

"No . . . not yet," she said reflexively.

"We're about to begin the shut-down process," the doctor said gently. "It's not going to get any easier."

Carol helped Eric rise from the chair. They shuffled over to the bed together and bent over their son's still form, kissing him good-bye for the last time. His body might as well have been a department store mannequin. For almost two years, they'd prayed that he'd come back, but now they had decided it was finally time to let go, time for him to go to a better place, where they might be reunited one day. Two children lost now.

The nurse switched off a machine, and the time between the beeps that indicated his lungs were inflating slowed. Then stopped. Another machine gurgled, then went quiet.

CHAPTER 55

IT DIDN'T TAKE LONG for Marshall and Mayberry to wake up, then walk to the vast meadow of tall green grass. Marshall pointed skyward. "Look."

A gray creature the size of a city bus was flying overhead, making a dusky blot against the blue sky. Within seconds, it disappeared into the distance.

Then an ear-piercing rumble shattered the quiet, and they felt a tremor pass under their feet.

Mayberry's face went pale. "That's a powerful earth spell being cast," she said, nervously rolling her shoulders forward.

"It came from that direction," Marshall said, pointing to a hillock about a hundred yards away. "That's where we left Aaron." He felt his own anxiety level shoot up four or five notches.

"We'd better get over there," Mayberry shouted as she started to sprint. "And fast."

Pulling up behind a large rock formation close to Aaron's cave, Marshall inhaled deeply before taking a look. A cacophony of thunderous noises rolled over the hill. He heard swords clashing and the battle cries of many species of warriors— all engaged in combat. Marshall steeled himself, then peered through a narrow cleft between the boulders. His eyes froze on a figure he never expected to see again. His heart began to hammer, and a brick grew and twisted in his gut.

Hurt, but very much alive, it was their malevolent nemesis . . . Monga. Dripping stumps were all that remained of his two left arms, a crudely attached wooden peg had replaced his right foreleg, and in lieu of his left eye, there remained only a fleshy, black, rotting hole. In spite of his misshapen appearance, he was as fearsome as ever, happily brutalizing a melee of Sleviccs with his magic assisted by an army of monsterous allies.

"There's Aaron," Mayberry said, stepping in next to Marshall and pointing to the top of the hill above the cave.

Heavy patches of sweat stained Aaron's shirt, his face was red and blotchy, and he stood on unsteady legs, leaning his shoulder into Uuth for balance. Kellain stood in front of Aaron protectively, valiantly shielding him from a gaggle of attacking Heeturs, the fierce-looking tattooed brick-colored creatures they'd seen marching by on the valley floor. Fighting like a Viking berserker, Kellain dispatched one Heetur after another with two-handed blows from his war club.

A gray wind spell dribbled from Aaron's fingers, but it wasn't strong enough to push back any of the attackers. Uuth's spiked tail flicked out viciously, administering a deathblow to one of the Heeturs' armored reptilian pets. The Heeturs had herded this group of Sleviccs into a circle, packing them together so tightly that it was becoming impossible for the Sleviccs to maneuver. It wouldn't be long before they were overrun and annihilated.

Hundreds of other Sleviccs were arrayed on the battlefield, fighting in military formations, each near the fluttering battle flags which identified their tribe. They fought valiantly against the undisciplined packs of Varnets and clumps of Heeturs besieging them.

At the far edge of the melee, Marshall spotted four huge creatures that he'd never seen before; they had large brown eyes, thick dark fur, and heads as big as desks. They lumbered forward, then sprung up on long legs, using their curved front claws to slash and rend a jumbled mass of Heeturs.

Another new species he saw in the fight was a pack of red-skinned beings with football-sized yellow eyes, who sped around on six legs, biting at the heels of Varnets. The Sleviccs had clearly allied with various other species to fight Monga and his army.

The entire battlefield was a nightmarish blur of slashing, thrusting, biting, and hammer blows.

A Heetur used one of its tusks to pierce a Slevicc's shin,

toppling it into a blob of Varnets. Without hesitating, a surge of Varnets leaped onto the Slevicc's back, merciless as army ants, and began stabbing her with small, flashing knives.

A small band of Sleviccs charged toward Monga, filling the air with the zing of tumbling axes and the whistle of spears. Monga raised a spiked wooden staff and used it to cast an orange defensive spell, creating an impenetrable force field that easily blasted the Sleviccs' weapons aside. He then fired an earth spell into the ground just ahead of his assailants, lifting tons of soil, rocks, and debris into the air, then releasing the detritus into the charging Sleviccs. Most of them were wounded or killed, as were a large number of Monga's own allies who weren't nimble—or smart—enough to get out of the way.

"Aaron's not dead yet," Marshall said, grimly trying to crystallize his thoughts and form a plan.

"*Yet* being the operative word," Mayberry replied, trailing her fingers over the rock.

Suddenly, Monga's staff shot an unrecognizable yellow spell at a gigantic Slevicc warrior who was demolishing his Heetur assailants with a long hammer. When the yellow spell struck his chest, the dumbfounded Slevicc froze in astonishment, as though he'd been zapped by a cattle prod. Then, a golden stream of energy began to flow from the Slevicc's body back into the spikes of Monga's staff. The Slevicc fell to his knees, then collapsed as his life force poured into Monga's staff. Yammering with excitement, three Heeturs jumped on top of the fallen Slevicc and began slashing.

Mayberry grabbed Marshall by the shoulders to force him to look at her. "Monga went back to the temple and found the wand. It *looks* like a staff, but I recognize the spell he just cast—it was one of the spells the wand etched in my mind."

CHAPTER 56

CAROL URGED THE NURSE to take Eric down the hall to the waiting room. If her husband stayed in the room any longer, she feared he would come apart, and she wouldn't be able to be put him back together again. Only one device was still operating, the pump in Aaron's chest that kept his lungs working. She searched her mind for the name of the device, but couldn't remember.

The nurse clicked a red lever to shut the pump off.

On the heart monitor's screen, a white line arced sharply upward, then began to flatten out, getting smaller and smaller.

She knew what that meant.

CHAPTER 57

MAYBERRY SEARCHED Marshall's eyes, ready for action but wanting to agree on a plan.

"The only way we can defeat him is if we launch a sneak attack before he knows we're here," Marshall said with a steely edge to his voice. "Hide behind that boulder for now. I'll circle around to his other side and creep in close. Wait until I attack. Then jump in. Once he's dead, the Sleviccs and their allies will help us deal with the pig-creatures and Heeturs."

Mayberry nodded and squeezed Marshall's hand, and they ran around the base of the hill. When Mayberry ducked behind the nearby boulder, her senses were in overdrive. She psyched herself up for one final battle with their remorseless foe. She knelt down to grab handfuls of the grass, scooping up rock and other debris, and stuffing all of it into her pockets. She was terrified. Fortunately, the hiding place Marshall had picked for her didn't intersect Monga's current kill zone.

Marshall was still on the move and had a ways to go. But when Mayberry peeked around the side of the boulder and saw more Sleviccs getting slaughtered, she was too brave and too impatient to wait for his signal. She invoked an earth spell, and waves of deep brown power poured from her fingers under the boulder. It shifted forward, jerked a few times, then tore itself from the ground, heading on a collision course with her target. The boulder thumped off Monga's exposed rear flank, driving him to his knees. The force of such a bone-crushing blow should have crippled or killed him. Instead, he wheeled on his haunches to face his new adversary. His nostrils flared as Mayberry hurled a series of fireballs at him. His staff's orange counterspell easily deflected her fireballs, which exploded above him like Fourth of July fireworks, lighting up the sky.

"Keedlun. Monga keel keedlun," he screeched, his face a murderous, foaming mask of bile, his one good eye as cold as ice.

A gray miasma wind spell exploded from his staff.

Mayberry had expected to be able to deflect his spell with one of her own, but Monga's jet of energy overwhelmed her defenses, hurling her body onto the turf. Cruelly bruised but with no bones broken, she scrambled to her feet, though the next power spell, which he had already fired her way, would probably finish her.

She was stupefied by what happened next. A luminescent bubble instantly appeared, enveloping her body just as Monga's enormous white miasma power spell struck. The spell bounced off her protective bubble, broke in two, flowed around it, and sped harmlessly past.

How am I doing this? Mayberry thought as she floated on her back in the bubble, perplexed. *This must be a protection spell Merlin's wand implanted in me when I controlled it.*

A bold Heetur charged Mayberry, battle-axe first, and leaped onto her bubble. His blow bounced off the orb like it was a rubber ball, and when his shoulder touched the bubble, he squealed, then dropped to the ground, unconscious. His scant hair stood straight out of his head, as if he'd touched a high-voltage electrified fence.

CHAPTER 58

MAYBERRY COULD SEE MONGA glaring ferociously at her only a hundred feet away. *What is Marshall doing? I should have waited.* Monga balanced his staff against his shoulder, grunting a spell while gesticulating with his upper right hand. He reached into one of his leather bags with his only other remaining hand and withdrew a pinch of purple powder. An ominous lavender glow began to swirl between his palms like a small tornado.

"*Keedlun die,*" he croaked.

The lavender cloud flew toward her bubble so fast that she barely had time to brace herself for its impact. Instead of smashing into the bubble, the cloud gently wafted through its skin, filling its interior with smoke, then coiled slowly around her body. For a second, it felt as though she was being immersed in scented lotion. Then the substance began to tighten around her. *Marshall, where are you?* She struggled for breath that wouldn't come because her diaphragm was being slowly crushed. Her eyes began to bulge from their sockets. The pain was agonizing, and her vision went fuzzy as her oxygen-starved brain slowed.

Hidden from the battlefield's carnage by the deep green grass, Marshall had crawled until he was just a few feet from Monga's blind side. He stopped and rolled up onto his hip, digging frantically in his backpack. Finally, he whipped out the revolver.

Marshall rocked to his feet—knees bent, body square to his target—and used both hands to aim the business end of the gun at the back of Monga's head. He scrunched his left eye shut as he focused on relaxing and pulling the trigger back, not too fast, not too slow.

No one could miss a target that big, this close.

Marshall squeezed the trigger three times in rapid succession, bracing for the explosive noise and recoil, followed by the splatter of Monga's blood. Instead of three loud bangs, the pistol expelled three sharp noises that sounded like a squeaky door. Stunned, Marshall lowered the tip of the barrel, watching the bullets transform into puffs of silver that burst softly on Monga's back before dissipating like glitter. He should have already learned this lesson. Earth technology didn't work on Nith.

Provoked by the strange sensations on his back, Monga swiveled his head, then glowered at Marshall with his flat, merciless eye. He whipped a tail around Marshall's waist and jerked him into the air, tilting his head forward to scrutinize him closer, all while still maintaining the lavender spell that was squeezing the life out of Mayberry.

Marshall's right hand was now only a few feet from the monster's face. Mustering the courage for one last roll of the dice, Marshall punched the pistol's steel barrel into the rotten black hole where Monga's eye had once resided.

Monga screamed and jerked his head down so violently it ripped the pistol out of Marshall's hand, rattling the nerves in his arm all the way up to his shoulder. The beast's tails went limp, and Marshall's body fell into the grass. Roaring like an angry lion, Monga plucked the gun barrel from his eye socket, then fell to the ground, where he released earsplitting screams of pain that reverberated across the whole battlefield.

The lavender cloud in Mayberry's bubble thinned and vanished.

Petrified by their master's unexpected change of fortune, the Varnets squealed, dropped their weapons, and fled, followed by the Heeturs, who immediately abandoned the fight with the exhausted Sleviccs.

Mayberry's lungs heaved, and her breath came back in staccato shudders as she struggled to recharge her brain and body. Her limbs tingled and burned as they woke up. She barely noticed when the bubble hit the ground and burst, flopping

Hurt, but very much alive, it was their malevolent nemesis . . . Monga.

her roughly onto the grass. Then she lifted her head and was surprised to see Mirrt blitzing across the meadow, with Co-Co riding on his right head.

Monga was still on the ground, writhing and screaming. The staff was lying near him untouched, only a few feet from his hands. Mayberry jumped up and sprinted for it.

Monga stopped screaming and summoned enough energy to desperately sweep the ground with his outstretched fingers to find the staff. Unfortunately, his hand touched the staff before Mayberry could reach it. He hoisted himself back onto his feet just as Mirrt leaped like a tiger, stretching open his cavernous, dagger-lined jaws. As Monga prepared to fire a power spell with the staff that would blow Mayberry into millions of pieces, Mirrt's right jaw clamped onto his wrist and nearly tore it apart, forcing him to release the staff.

With dazzling speed, Co-Co skipped off Mirrt's left head and used her tail to snatch the staff out of midair and flick it to Mayberry, who caught the magical artifact in her palm, right where it belonged.

Co-Co inflated her body as she tumbled down. She resembled a furry beach ball that bobbed gently in the air.

As Monga's staff morphed into Merlin's wand, the runes inscribed on it glowed a bright yellow, infusing Mayberry with a tremendous surge of energy. A nanosecond later, she fired the yellow spell into Monga's chest. The spell paralyzed the pitiful remains of his broken body, and then a golden stream of energy began to flow out of Monga's massive torso and back into the wand, quickly turning from trickle to torrent.

Monga collapsed into a mountainous flaccid heap. One of his hands clawed spastically at the air while the other fell limply into the ground.

Game over.

CHAPTER 59

CO-CO DRIFTED TO THE GROUND, extended her feet, and gently touched down. She expelled the excess air from her body and pranced merrily over to Mayberry's side.

Mayberry absorbed as much of the wand's stolen energy as her body would allow. She gazed around and suddenly knew what she had to do. Leveling the wand, she pushed out golden streams of energy into the wounded and dying Sleviccs and their allies, who littered the battlefield. The warriors instantly began to revive.

One by one, they sat up and tested out their limbs, trying to fathom what had happened and amazed that certain death had turned into renewed strength and miraculous healing. Finally, they gathered at a respectful distance in a happy jostling crowd to salute Mayberry.

Kellain began to chant her name slowly, and the other Sleviccs joined in. "Mayberry, Mayberry, Mayberry," they yelled lustily, then bowed their heads as if she were the queen of Nith.

"Mayberry," Marshall shouted with a big smile, "it looks like the Sleviccs are finally ready to give you the throne." Then his eyes went wide and he turned to point at their helpless friend. "Aaron. Use the wand on Aaron."

Jolted back to reality, Mayberry spun around and trained the wand on Aaron, who was now lying on his back near the cave's mouth. They ran to his side and touched his clammy face. His breath was barely a whisper, his face eggshell white. Mayberry used the wand to pour streams of golden life force into him.

He didn't revive.

"This should have healed him," Mayberry said, her eyes pooling with tears.

"I'm dying," Aaron gurgled, his eyes still closed. "Thank you for coming back. You saved us. Well, most . . . of . . . us."

"Don't give up," Marshall said, grasping his hand. "We are going to take you back to Earth. Your parents don't blame you for Laura's death. They love you, and they need you to come home."

Aaron's eyelids fluttered, then glazed over and stared blankly at the sky. Marshall took his pulse; it was very faint.

"He's unconscious but breathing," Marshall said. "Let's move. The doctors on Earth must have already pulled the plug. Otherwise your spell would have healed him."

Mayberry unconsciously slid the wand into her backpack, put it on, and then reached down to grab Aaron under the arm. As Marshall reached for his other arm, Kellain shook his head, then picked Aaron up like he weighed nothing and threw his limp body over a shoulder. Together, they sprinted toward the grove. When they hit the forest's edge, Kellain mewed and looked concerned, but he kept moving into it anyway.

Co-Co, Mirrt, and Uuth remained where they were, watching.

When they finally reached the Tree, Kellain gently laid Aaron's body next to its trunk. He touched Aaron's chest and forehead with his fingertips, bowed his head, and waved good-bye. Then he turned and loped away.

Marshall and Mayberry quickly flopped down to flank Aaron and touched his hands.

"All three of us want to go back to Earth *together*," both of them said, their voices tight.

Aaron's ragged breathing suddenly stopped. As he dreamed of home, a vortex of white light grew brighter and bigger, beckoning his soul into it . . .

CHAPTER 60

MARSHALL'S EYES FLUTTERED OPEN, and he jerked upright. Mayberry was still sleeping, so he shook her shoulders gently to wake her up. The sun had set and it was pitch-black.

"Where's Aaron?" Mayberry asked, before her eyes were even all the way open. "Were we too late?"

"If he's alive, he's at the hospital," Marshall said.

"Right. You're right," she said, then sat up and gazed into the woods, and at the backpack, which lay by her side. "Oh my God," she breathed. "Look at this," she said, pulling the wand from the back pocket of her pack. It didn't look impressive—it really did look like an ordinary brown stick—but its power pulsed through her hand. Mayberry tried a simple fire spell.

It worked. A bright white beam of light spat from the end of the wand, lighting up the whole area around them.

"Ha! For once we don't have to find our way out of here in the dark," Mayberry said, grinning like a circus clown.

Marshall was tingling with excitement. "The Tree brought back a material object from Nith. That proves that it exists on a *physical* plane, not just a mental one."

"As if there was any doubt about *that*," Mayberry said, staring at the light coming from the wand's tip. "People have definitely used the wand on Earth—look at Merlin. But I don't think we want anyone here in this era learning how to use it. Too many crazies."

"I agree," Marshall said, nodding. "That wand can't fall into the wrong hands—look at what happened when Monga had it. So we can't tell *anybody* about it. Or about the Wishing Tree," Marshall said, shaking his head sadly.

"We're the only people on Earth who can do actual magic. We'd be *superstars* if people knew."

Mayberry dusted the leaves and brush from her sweater. "Let's forget about that for now and find Aaron."

Later, after they exited the forest and started walking through the meadow, Marshall whipped out his cell phone—7:35 P.M. He went online and looked up the number for Methodist United Hospital, then clicked on the number.

After he was put through, he immediately asked the nurse on duty whether Aaron Fitzsimmons was still alive, then nodded and hung up.

"He's *alive* and *awake* in room 1424. We *did it!*" he said, grabbing Mayberry and pulling her into a tight hug.

"What are we waiting for?" Mayberry said, her face flushed with excitement. "We can ride to the hospital. If we pedal fast, it shouldn't take more than half an hour."

CHAPTER 61

THEY SLIPPED OFF THE ELEVATOR on Aaron's floor. The nurses seated behind the floor's reception cubicle were being inundated by phone calls. The word was out. A miracle had occurred. The boy who had been in a coma had woken up just as he was being pulled off life support.

Marshall and Mayberry scurried past the busy nurses' station toward room 1424. When they got there, Mayberry poked her head through the open door to peek into Aaron's room. Aaron was sitting up, clad in a standard pale green hospital gown, with his legs dangling loosely over the side of his bed. He looked bright-eyed and chipper.

Two doctors hovered nearby as a third slid a stethoscope over his chest.

The depth of the emotion floating in the room was overwhelming. Aaron's mother's face was streaked with tears of relief. His father wore a huge lopsided grin and couldn't stop patting his wife's head and shoulders.

The doctor with the stethoscope glared imperiously at Mayberry when he spotted her. *"Excuse me,"* he said, making a sweeping motion with a hand. "You're not allowed in here."

"But—" Mayberry began as Marshall stepped up beside her.

"Mayberry!" Aaron shouted with glee, sliding off the bed. "Marshall. Look at me. I'm *fourteen.*"

"But . . . but . . . you have to stay in bed," the flustered doctor blurted out. He reached to push the boy back, but Aaron deftly maneuvered around him with a grace and vigor that clearly shocked the doctors.

"I've been in bed long enough," he declared. "I need to see my friends now."

He flew across the room on bare feet, with the back of his green hospital gown flapping behind him. First he embraced Mayberry, then Marshall.

"Aaron," the doctor sharply commanded, "these visitors need to leave. There are rules in this ward, and we have a number of tests to run. We need to determine how—"

"I expect you'll have to do those tests, but not until Aaron's ready," said Eric in a gruff baritone. "A miracle saved my boy, and if he wants to see his friends, you're not going to stop him."

Aaron's mom lifted her head and narrowed her eyes at the flustered doctor and his companions. "You told me to let my boy go, and he was alive. You know what? Get out. I don't want to see any of you in here again."

EPILOGUE

Two Months Later . . .

THE MOST POPULAR STUDENT at Eden Grove High School strolled down the school's main hall, surrounded by a fleet of admirers. Aaron was the first celebrity that Eden Grove had ever produced. After the story of his incredible recovery broke, the rabid press nicknamed him Miracle Boy, and it stuck. His remarkable poise and strikingly mature responses to the media's questions sealed his rock star status. He claimed to have no idea how or why his miracle had occurred, but that didn't matter; the frenzy continued unabated. Every entertainment outlet wanted a piece of this feelgood story, especially because it was also tinged by the tragic death of a little girl. The mystery surrounding his remarkable recovery *after* his plug was pulled deepened when he refused to submit to any further medical examinations.

Aaron high-fived Marshall and winked at Mayberry as he cruised by his best friends.

Some of the girls at school now tried to emulate bits and pieces of Mayberry's eclectic style—even going as far as dying their hair with bright streaks of color. So many classmates were trying to "friend" Mayberry that she couldn't keep up.

"See you after class," Marshall said, giving Mayberry's waist a squeeze. "By the way, I'm writing a book titled *How My Girlfriend and I Found an Ancient Sentient Tree That Teleported Us to Another Universe to Rescue a Boy Presumed Brain-Dead.* Kind of catchy, isn't it?"

She shook her head and laughed, then went up on tiptoe to give him a kiss.

"You know, Marshall, now that we've confirmed the greatest scientific discovery in human history, we need to find another project to research—like why those sealed bags of salad turn brown the second you get them home."

Marshall chuckled, then turned away and walked toward his English class.

Whap.

He felt a light burning sensation between his shoulder blades. He whipped his head around and saw that Mayberry was also reaching for Monga's mark. Farther down the hall, Aaron was doing the same.

As the threesome felt their marks light up at school, Merlin's wand—stashed in Mayberry's bedroom closet at home—popped straight up into the air and began spitting yellow sparks. It started to rotate, faster and faster, transforming into Excalibur, then Thor's hammer, then the Cup of Jamshid, then another object of power, and another until it was just a wild blur of constant motion.

Simultaneously, the walking stick marked MF CENTER 1 floated into the air next to the wand spitting yellow sparks too, spinning slowly at first, then speeding up and transforming into different objects of power, just like its neighbor.

Poof.

Marshall, Mayberry, and Aaron felt the burning sensations on their backs ease.

The power objects slowed. Floating back to the closet floor, they reverted to their original forms: a walking stick and an innocuous-looking wand. Without a master to command their power, they were merely branches cut from the Wishing Tree, centuries apart.

Marshall caught Mayberry's eye. She touched her mark and shrugged. He shrugged back, gave a thumbs-up to her and Aaron, then kept walking to class.

BIBLIOGRAPHY

Cox, Brian, and Andrew Cohen. *Wonders of Life: Exploring the Most Extraordinary Phenomenon in the Universe.* New York: Harper Design, 2013.

DiChristina, Mariette, ed. "Extreme Physics: Probing the Mysteries of the Cosmos." Special Collector's Edition, *Scientific American,* Summer 2013.

Mitton, Jeffry B., and Michael C. Grant. "Genetic Variation and the Natural History of Quaking Aspen." *BioScience* 46, no. 1 (January 1996): 25–31.

Quammen, David. "The World's Largest Trees." *National Geographic,* December 2012.

Steinhardt, Paul J., and Neil Turok. *Endless Universe: Beyond the Big Bang.* New York: Doubleday, 2007.